PRAISE

D0962718

HARLEY QUINN BREAKING GLASS

A GRAPHIC NOVEL

"The fast-paced plot enhanced by Harley's trademark style of speech examines the impact of gentrification, and Harley's character development follows a redemptive arc that will have readers rooting for her and her colorful family."
—**KIRKUS REVIEWS**

"Breaking Glass is a standout achievement that demonstrates the unique blend of words, pictures, and color that comics offer."
—**FOREWORD REVIEWS**

"Mariko Tamaki's voice is absolute perfection in this altogether refreshing spin on a young Harleen Quinzel's beginnings. Anchored by stunning art by Steve Pugh, readers get to revel in a Gotham City that has drag queens fighting gentrification, a familiar-named practical activist going against an all-consuming corporation, and an endearing delinquent just trying to find the fairy tale that fits her remarkable life. Shantay, you stay (on my bookshelf for decades to come), *Breaking Glass.*"
—**SINA GRACE, GLAAD MEDIA AWARD NOMINATED AUTHOR OF *ICEMAN***

HARLEY QUINN
BREAKING GLASS

A GRAPHIC NOVEL

WRITTEN BY

mariko tamaki

ART BY

steve pugh

LETTERED BY

carlos m. mangual

MARIE JAVINS Editor
DIEGO LOPEZ Assistant Editor
STEVE COOK Design Director - Books
AMIE BROCKWAY-METCALF Publication Design

BOB HARRAS Senior VP - Editor-in-Chief, DC Comics
MICHELE R. WELLS VP & Executive Editor, Young Reader

DAN DiDIO Publisher
JIM LEE Publisher & Chief Creative Officer
BOBBIE CHASE VP - New Publishing Initiatives & Talent Development
DON FALLETTI VP - Manufacturing Operations & Workflow Management
LAWRENCE GANEM VP - Talent Services
ALISON GILL Senior VP - Manufacturing & Operations
HANK KANALZ Senior VP - Publishing Strategy & Support Services
DAN MIRON VP - Publishing Operations
NICK J. NAPOLITANO VP - Manufacturing Administration & Design
NANCY SPEARS VP - Sales

HARLEY QUINN: BREAKING GLASS

Published by DC Comics. Copyright © 2019 DC Comics. All Rights Reserved. All characters, their distinctive likenesses and related elements featured in this publication are trademarks of DC Comics. DC INK is a trademark of DC Comics. The stories, characters and incidents featured in this publication are entirely fictional. DC Comics does not read or accept unsolicited submissions of ideas, stories or artwork.

DC - a WarnerMedia Company.

DC Comics, 2900 West Alameda Ave.
Burbank, CA 91505

Printed by LSC Communications, Crawfordsville, IN, USA. 7/26/19. First printing.

ISBN: 978-1-4012-8329-2

Library of Congress Cataloging-in-Publication Data

Names: Tamaki, Mariko, author.
Title: Harley Quinn : breaking glass : a graphic novel / Mariko Tamaki ; illustrated by Steve Pugh.
Other titles: Breaking glass
Description: Burbank : DC Ink, 2019.
Identifiers: LCCN 2019012179 | ISBN 9781401283292 (paperback)
Subjects: LCSH: Graphic novels.
Classification: LCC PZ7.7.T355 Har 2019 | DDC 741.5/973--dc23

TABLE OF CONTENTS

CHAPTER ONE

LISTEN UP, 'CUZ I'M GONNA TELL YOU THIS REALLY GREAT STORY AND YOU'RE GONNA LOVE IT. IT'S GONNA MAKE YOUR BRAINS EXPLODE LIKE SPAGHETTI.
READY?
OKAY. NO INTERRUPTING!
OKAY.
ONCE UPON A TIME, NOT SO SO LONG AGO, THERE WAS A MOST AMAZING PERSON...

...WHO WAS FROM EVERYWHERE AND NOWHERE.
AND HER NAME WAS...
TA-DA!
HARLEEN QUINZEL.
OKAY YEAH, IT'S ME.
GOOD GUESS, SMARTY FACE. STOP INTERRUPTING ALREADY.
WHO ELSE IS THERE?
GOTHAM
THAT'S THE LADY WHO SPENT FIVE HOURS SINGING "YOU BELONG WITH ME" ON THE BUS.
DON'T KNOW WHO THAT GUY IS. HE'S NOT PART OF THE STORY. IGNORE HIM.
ANYWAY!
HARLEEN WAS NOT OBVIOUSLY THE KIND OF PERSON WHO A FAIRY TALE-TYPE STORY IS ABOUT.

'CUZ MOSTLY SHE WAS JUST THE KIND OF PERSON WITH A KNAPSACK AND FIVE BUCKS.
WHAT CAN I GET YOU?
YOU GOT CEREAL?
THREE FORTY-FIVE TO GOTHAM IS LEAVING IN FIVE!
AH NUTS. NEVER MIND.
HEY, KID.
CATCH!
THANKS, MA'AM!
HARLEEN WAS REALLY GOOD AT BEING THE KIND OF PERSON WITH A KNAPSACK AND FIVE BUCKS, SO IT WAS NO BIG THING.
SO ANYWAY, AT THIS, THE BEGINNING PART OF THE STORY, HARLEEN WAS ON HER WAY...

...TO GRANDMOTHER'S HOUSE.
GET IT? LIKE IN THE FAIRY TALE!
HOLY BUNNY SLIPPERS, LOOK AT THAT.
EXCEPT IN THIS STORY, GRANDMOTHER'S HOUSE WAS IN THE ONE AND ONLY...
...GOTHAM CITY!
OOOOOOOOO...
FOR THOSE OF YOU WHO DON'T KNOW, GOTHAM CITY IS KIND OF LIKE THIS OOO-LA-LA FANCY PLACE WHERE MANY FAMOUS INFAMOUS TYPES LIVE.
FROM THE WAY, WAY OUTSIDE, GOTHAM LOOKS LIKE...
...LIKE BUILDING BUILDING BUILDING REALLY BIG BUILDING BUILDING BUILDING-TYPE THING.

UP CLOSE, IN SOME OF THE UNDER-UNDER PARTS, IT'S KINDA A MESS.
SMELLS LIKE ARMPIT AND LIPSTICK.
IN "LITTLE RED RIDING HOOD," THE GRANDMA GETS EATEN. SPOILER ALERT! WHICH IS KINDA GROSS. ESPECIALLY IF YOU LIKE GRANDMOTHERS.
HARLEEN ALWAYS THOUGHT IT WAS A BUMMER THAT A LUMBERJACK HAD TO SAVE LITTLE RED RIDING HOOD.
HARLEEN WOULD HAVE JUST PUNCHED THE WOLF IN THE FACE.
CLICK!
NO LUMBERJACK REQUIRED.

HELLO? UH. GRANDMOTHER?
HARLEEN'S MOM HADN'T SEEN HER MOM IN A LONG, LONG TIME. SO IT WAS A BIT OF A RISK SENDING HER ONLY KID ALL THE WAY TO GOTHAM FOR A YEAR WHILE SHE WENT TO WORK FOR CHERRY CRUISES, THE SWEETEST CRUISES IN THE WORLD.
HEY, UH, IT'S HARLEEN? MOM WROTE AND SAID I WAS COMING?
COOL OLD-PEOPLE STUFF.
WELL, HELLO THERE. CAN I HELP YOU?
YOU LOOK LIKE YOU JUST ROLLED OFF A BUS.
MAMA, A.K.A. BENNY, A.K.A. THE FAIRY GODPERSON OF THE STORY, A.K.A. YES, I KNOW LITTLE RED RIDING HOOD DOESN'T HAVE A FAIRY GODPERSON, SHUT UP.
TURNS OUT HARLEEN'S MOM SHOULD HAVE KEPT BETTER TRACK OF HER MOTHER.

GOTHAM CITY
I AM SORRY ABOUT YOUR GRANDMA, KIDDO. I WON'T LIE, IT WAS A SMALL FUNERAL.
MAMA GETS TO BE THE FAIRY GODPERSON OF THE STORY BECAUSE HE SAID HE IS A FAIRY AND BECAUSE HE IS THE MOST NON-BOOGER PERSON IN ANY STORY EVER.
THANKS. I'M SORRY I MISSED IT. I MEAN, I DIDN'T REALLY KNOW HER.
WELL, SHE WAS A NICE LADY WHO STILL LIKED ELVIS. WHICH IS AN ADMIRABLE THING, I SUPPOSE. NOT THAT I LIKE ELVIS.
MAMA SAID YOU COULD CALL HIM A FAIRY OR YOU COULD CALL HIM A CAB.
ALSO A BIT OF A CLOWN FANATIC, WHICH I ALWAYS ENJOYED.
S'WHAT DO WE DO NOW, KIDDO? SOCIAL SERVICES?
UH!

AW GEE, CAT WHISKERS, MISS MA'AM. CAN I STAY, PLEASE, PLEASE? I'LL GET A JOB. ANYTHING! AW PLEASE?
MISS MA'AM! WELL THAT'S SOME-THING.
A NON-FAIRY-GODPERSON TYPE PROBABLY WOULD HAVE CALLED THE AUTHORIZED AUTHORITIES OR SOMETHING.

PLEASE, PLEASE, PLEASE, PLEASE WITH A BUCKET OF COCOA PUFFS ON TOP, MS. BENNY?
FIRST, I'M MAMA TO MY FRIENDS, BUT A PROUD GAY MAN, SO JUST MAMA WILL DO FINE.

SECOND, YOU DON'T LOOK CUT OUT FOR HARD LABOR, KIDDO.

AND I DON'T THINK THAT CHILD SERVICES SYSTEM HELPS ANYONE THESE DAYS.
YOUR GRANDMA HAD A BIG WIN WITH HER "SCRATCHERS" LAST MONTH AND SHE'D PAID UP HER RENT FOR A WHILE.
AND SINCE I'M THE MANAGER OF THIS BUILDING... I SAY YOU STAY. JUST...

...GO TO SCHOOL, STAY CUTE, AND DON'T GET INTO ANY TROUBLE.

WE'LL KEEP YOU FED AND CLOTHED.
ALL I EAT IS HOT DOGS, CANDY BARS, AND CEREAL.
HOW QUAINT.
THANK YOU, THANK YOU, THANK YOU, THANK YOU.
HARLEEN'S MOM TOLD HER ONCE THAT THERE ARE DEVILS AND THERE ARE ANGELS.
THE CURE MIX
A DEVIL SHOT HARLEEN'S FATHER WHEN SHE WAS FOUR YEARS OLD, IN THE PARKING LOT OF A GULP 'N' GAS.
HARLEEN'S FATHER, DASH ALABASTER QUINZEL, WAS AN ANGEL WHO NEVER SWORE AND WAS GOING TO BUY HIS FAMILY A HOUSE WITH AN ALLIGATOR SLIDE AND A DOUGHNUT FLOATY.

A DEVIL STOLE THE QUINZEL-MOBILE ON HARLEEN'S TENTH BIRTHDAY, RIGHT OUTSIDE BINGO BETTY'S BONKERS ARCADE.
LET'S GO!
NO.
PIZZA
GAMES
HEY!
DAMMIT!
NO YOU DON'T, YOU BOOGER!
LET'S GO, DUDE!
HARLEEN CHASED 'EM.
SQUEEE
HARLEEEN! HARLEEN, STOP!
BUT THE DEVIL GOT AWAY.
ESCAPED WITH HIS WINGED MAN.

HARLEEN!
YOU BOOGERS!
SQUEEEEEE
THIS IS WHERE OUR YOUNG HARLEEN FIRST HAD THE THOUGHT THAT MAYBE THERE ARE NOT A LOT OF ANGELS IN THIS WORLD.

BEEP! BEEP!
BECAUSE HARLEEN HAD LIVED IN MANY PLACES, IT DID NOT TAKE HER LONG TO GET SETTLED.
07:24
BEEP!
HARLEEN HAD ONCE LIVED IN A TOWN ACTUALLY CALLED PUTTHOLE.
SLAM!
IF YOU CAN LIVE IN A CITY CALLED PUTTHOLE...
...YOU CAN LIVE ANYWHERE.
HAVE A FABULOUS DAY, KIDDO!
LATER, MAMA!
For Sale
555-100
HERE IS HARLEEN'S GUIDE TO MOST IMPORTANT THINGS TO HAVE WHERE YOU LIVE, WHEREVER THAT IS.

NUMBA ONE! GOTTA GET A GOOD COFFEE PLACE.
THERE YOU GO.
THANKS, MISTER!
NO ONE SHOULD PAY MORE THAN A BUCK FOR A COFFEE. THAT'S STRAIGHT-UP **HIGHWAY STEALING** OR SOMETHING.

NUMBA TWO! HOT DOG PLACE.
MUSTARD AND KETCHUP?
YUP!

NUMBA THREE! A NICE, COZY BREAKFAST SPOT WITH A GOOD VIEW.
SUUUUUUNNY DAY!

THESE ARE THE THINGS THAT MAKE LIFE AWESOME NO MATTER WHERE YOU ARE.

EVEN IF WHERE YOU ARE IS...

...GOTHAM HIGH.
DUN DUN DUN!
NAH, I'M JUST KIDDIN', IT'S JUST A HIGH SCHOOL. NO BIGS.
GOTHAM HIGH WAS A LAND OF LOTS O' RICH KIDS AND POOR KIDS AND WEIRDOS AND JOCKS AND KIDS WHO ARE OBSESSED WITH THEIR PHONES AND WEAR EXPENSIVE T-SHIRTS THAT SMELL LIKE THE MALL.
LIKE THIS GUY.
BRIIIING!
ANYWAY, WHERE WAS I?
OH RIGHT, HIGH SCHOOL.
HIGH SCHOOL IS SO...HIGH SCHOOL.
ARE THERE ANY PEOPLE OUT THERE WHO ACTUALLY LIKE HIGH SCHOOL?
I MEAN, CAN YOU ACTUALLY LIKE HIGH SCHOOL THE WAY YOU LIKE A DOUGHNUT OR A PUPPY?
I DON'T THINK SO.

SO IT WAS ON THIS, HER SECOND DAY AT SCHOOL, THAT FAIR HARLEEN CONFIRMED THAT GOTHAM HIGH, LIKE ALL SCHOOLS, WAS MOSTLY FULL OF BOOGERS.
A BOOGER IS A PERSON WHO ACTS LIKE A BOOGER.
LIKE THIS GUY.
SLAM
HEY!
WAY TO BE A HIGH SCHOOL STEREOTYPE!
CREEP.
GUH.
MOST HIGH SCHOOLS ARE ABOUT EIGHTY PERCENT BOOGERS.
THAT'S JUST SCIENTIFIC-TYPE STUFF.
HANG IN THERE, TODD.
YEAH. THANKS, IVY.
HALF OF HIGH SCHOOL IS LEARNING HOW TO DEAL WITH BOOGERS.

STUDENTS! TAKE YOUR SEATS.
I SAID, TAKE YOUR SEATS!
IN THE OTHER HALF, YOU LEARN ABOUT THIS OLD GUY WHO WROTE PLAYS ABOUT SAD PEOPLE WHO USED TEN WORDS WHEN TWO WERE TOTALLY GOOD.
IN THE OTHER HALF HALF, THE ALL-IMPORTANT THIRD HALF HALF HALF, YOU TRY TO MEET NEW AND INTERESTING PEOPLE TYPES.
YES?
HI! I'M HARLEEN!
OKAY.
YOU'RE IN MY MATH CLASS AND MY CHEMISTRY CLASS AND MY ENGLISH CLASS.
THAT'S RIGHT.
YOU'RE IVY, RIGHT?
I AM.
PLANT NAMES ARE COOL.

THANKS.
YEAH.
SO. READING, HUH?
YOU GOT SOMETHING AGAINST BOOKS?
ME? MOI?! WHY WOULD I HAVE SOMETHING AGAINST BOOKS? WHAT AM I, A BOOK HATER OR SOMETHIN'?
NO. I JUST-- WHATEVER. SORRY.
IT'S A BOOK ABOUT POLITICS.
COOOOOOL.
LESS TALKING, MORE READING! WE'RE GOING TO START TODAY WITH "THE LOTTERY"--
FROM THE MOMENT HARLEEN MET IVY...
...SHE KNEW IVY WAS A SUPER-SPECIAL PERSON.

HOW CAN WE TALK ABOUT GLOBAL WARMING WITHOUT TALKING ABOUT HUMAN BEHAVIOR?
IVY WAS ONE OF THOSE PEOPLE WHO ALWAYS HAD QUESTIONS.
ARE WE VIEWING THIS ISSUE INTERSECTIONALLY? BECAUSE I DON'T THINK WE CAN TALK ABOUT CLASS WITHOUT TALKING ABOUT RACE AND GENDER.
MOSTLY, IVY HAD ALL THIS STUFF SHE WANTED TO TALK ABOUT...
ARE WE SERIOUSLY STILL CUTTING INTO INNOCENT CREATURES IN THE NAME OF "LEARNING ABOUT BIOLOGY"?
...THAT OTHER PEOPLE WEREN'T TALKING ABOUT.
GAWD. GAG. JUST GET OVER IT ALREADY.
EVEN WHEN IT BUGGED OTHER PEOPLE.
IVY DIDN'T CARE.
WHICH WAS COOL.
SUPER COOL.

THE BEST THING TO DO WITH A SUPER-SPECIAL PERSON IS TO MAKE THEM YOUR FRIEND.
SO THAT'S WHAT HARLEEN DID.
HI!
GAH!
SO. WHAT'S FOR LUNCH?
A BEAN SALAD. MY BEAN SALAD.
AND WHAT ARE YOU HAVING?
TA-DA!
ARE YOU SERIOUS? THAT'S YOUR LUNCH? THAT'S A CHOCOLATE BAR.
IT'S A CHOCOLATE AND PEANUT CRUNCH. THE NUTS ARE FOR IRON.
MEGA PEANUT CRUNCHY
SO...
ARE WE FRIENDS NOW OR WHAT?

I DON'T EVEN KNOW YOU.
YEAH, 'CUZ WE JUST MET. 'CUZ I'M NEW HERE.
YEAH?
WHERE ARE YOU FROM?
SO I WAS BORN IN THIS LITTLE TRAILER PARK CALLED ***THE LITTLE TRAILER PARK***, AND MY ***MOM*** SAID WHEN I WAS BORN I WAS AS BIG AS A PEACH AND JUST AS SWEET. 'KAY, SO THEN I TURNED ***ONE*** AND...

YOU KNOW THAT FEELING OF, LIKE, PRETTY MUCH ALMOST COMPLETELY AND ABSOLUTELY PERFECT HAPPY?
LIKE THE FIRST TIME YOU HEAR A REALLY GOOD SONG THAT'S ABOUT TO BE YOUR FAVORITE SONG?
LIKE ICE CREAM THAT'S JUST BEEN SCOOPED AND STILL LOOKS LIKE A PICTURE OF ICE CREAM?
FUTURE SITE OF
STACK-MART
STACK-MART
KANE PROPERTY
SUUUUUUNNY DAY!
COFFEE
Coffee Toff
MMMM MMM MM.
Coffee-lat

FRESH-OUT-OF THE-CELLOPHANE-HAPPINESS.
HEY! KIDDO!
YA! WHAT?!
SHOW STARTS IN FIVE MINUTES!
HEY, DANIEL!
HEY, BARNEY!
HEY, MAX!
HEY, MARK!
HAVE A SEAT!
HEY, HARLEEN!

I THINK I SHOULD JUST SHAVE THEM.
JUST DO IT AND SHUT UP ABOUT IT.
LOOK AT THIS IDIOT. BIDDING FIFTY DOLLARS ON A VACUUM?
WHY DO GAME-SHOW DUDES ALWAYS HAVE HELMET HAIR?
EVERY-ONE BE QUIET, I CAN'T HEAR A THING.
AND YES INDEED, OUR HAPPY HEROINE HARLEEN WAS HAPPY AS A KITTEN ON A RADIATOR.
SHE HAD EVERYTHING SHE NEEDED.

A NEW VEGETARIAN BEST FRIEND.

IT'S TRULY UNBELIEVABLE THE GARBAGE CORPORATE CHAINS TRY TO PASS OFF AS FOOD IN THIS CITY.

WONDER WHAT IT'S LIKE TO HAVE AN EXTRA NOSTRIL.

AND A MUTINY OF QUEENS.

THAT'S WHAT DALI SAID IT WAS CALLED.

SO ALL YOU DO ALL NIGHT IS PRETEND TO SING SONGS AND WEAR LOTS OF MAKE-UP AND DRESSES AND GLITTER AND STUFF?

I KNOW, RIGHT? GOOD THING IT DOESN'T PAY.

WHAT WE DO IS **ART**, SWEETHEART. ***A.R.T.***

MAMA'S PROUDLY PRESENTS...

HELLO DALI!

BETTY COUP!

MIA CULPA!

AND MAXIMA IMPACT!

WHAT COULD GO WRONG?

MaMa's

CHAPTER TWO

I'M NOT SAYING WRONG. I'M SAYING THERE'S A STATE OF INEQUALITY. THE WORLD IS AN UNFAIR PLACE, ALL THE TIME.
ALL THE TIME? THAT'S A LOTTA TIME.
ALL THE TIME.
LIKE, TAKE THIS.
THIS IS FILM CLUB, RIGHT? SCHOOL CLUB. AND YET!
THIS CLUB HAS NEVER PLAYED A MOVIE DIRECTED BY A WOMAN. LET ALONE A WOMAN OF COLOR.
FILM CLUB
NAME ME A FILM DIRECTED BY A FEMALE THAT IS WORTHY OF DISCUSSION, MISS IVY. I'M ALL EARS.
WHALE RIDER. PARIAH. THE HURT LOCKER. THE BABADOOK...
JOHN KANE LOOKED LIKE AN AD FOR A BLAZER.
A PLEASURE TO MEET YOU. I'M JOHN KANE.
DON'T BRING YOUR TIRED DIVERSITY AGENDA TO MY ARENA. IT'S POINTLESS.
GUY WAS LIKE A HUMAN NECKTIE.

GEEZ.
DID HE JUST SAY "MY ARENA" TO ME?
THAT GUY IS A BOOG--
HARLEEN THOUGHT MAYBE JOHN KANE WAS A PERSON A LOT OF PEOPLE THOUGHT ABOUT DECKING.
SCREW YOU!
JUST BECAUSE YOUR PARENTS OWN GOTHAM DOESN'T MEAN YOU GET TO USE YOUR PATRIARCHAL SUB-STANDARDS TO DEFINE ART! DICK!
GUYS LIKE THAT, ALL YOU REALLY NEED TO DO TO THEM IS TAKE AWAY THEIR PHONES. THEY HATE THAT. ALSO, THEN YOU GET A NEW PHONE.
YOU KNOW WHAT?
YOU WANT TO DRAW GROSS THINGS ON ALL THE POSTERS? I HAVE A MARKER!
FILM CLUB
THE HISTORY OF WOMEN IN THE WORLD OF THE ARTS IS A HISTORY OF EXCLUSION AND WE ARE NOT GOING TO TAKE IT ANYMORE!

CITY COUNCILOR CORRINE DU, A.K.A. IVY'S MOM.

BECAUSE THIS IS OUR COMMUNITY! THIS IS OUR HOME! WE ARE **NOT** GOING AWAY. WE ARE NOT GOING TO BE DRIVEN OUT BY THE CORPORATE POWERS THAT BE.

WE KNOW OUR RIGHTS.

IVY'S MOM DIDN'T BELIEVE IN DEVILS OR ANGELS. SHE BELIEVED IN **RIGHTS.**

WE ARE READY FOR THIS **FIGHT.**

CLAP

CLAP

YOUR MOM IS SOOOO AWESOME.

MY MOM KICKS SERIOUS ASS.

CLAP

CLAP

CLAP

CLAP

MOM, DAD, THIS IS HARLEEN. SHE JUST MOVED HERE.
HI, IVY'S PARENTS!
WELCOME TO THE NEIGHBORHOOD, HARLEEN. THANKS FOR COMING.

THESE ARE FLYERS FOR YOUR FAMILY. ABOUT THE DEVELOPERS. OKAY?
I'LL GIVE 'EM TO MAMA!

MY DAD OWNS THE ONLY LOCAL GROCER IN THE NEIGHBORHOOD.
AND HE RUNS THE COMMUNITY GARDEN THAT I WORK AT.
SO MY LIFE IS KIND OF, YOU KNOW, COMMUNITY-ACTIVISM STUFF ALL THE TIME.
HIPPIE STUFF?
ONE, IT'S NOT HIPPIE STUFF, IT'S ABOUT LOOKING AFTER YOUR COMMUNITY AND THEIR RIGHTS. TWO, THERE'S ACTUALLY NOTHING WRONG WITH HIPPIE STUFF, OKAY?
GOTCHA.
WELL, LOOK WHO'S HERE.
WHO? THE GUY IN THE HAT? THAT'S A NICE HAT.
NO. THE KANES. MILLENNIUM ENTERPRISES.
HOW COME THEIR COFFEES ARE SO BIG?
BECAUSE THEY'RE ASSHOLES.

HEY, MAMA! I WENT TO THIS NEIGHBORHOOD THING WITH MY NEW FRIEND IVY WHO'S KIND OF A HIPPIE AND THAT'S A GOOD THING FOR THE COMMUNITY AND HER MOM GAVE ME SOME FLYERS FOR YOU.

HEY, KIDDO.

YOU GET DINNER YET? SHOULD WE COOK UP SOME CEREAL FOR YOU?

WHOSE COFFEE IS THAT?

THAT, SWEET GIRL, IS THE DEVIL'S COFFEE.

WHAT'S THE LETTER FOR?

THEY'RE TRYING TO GET RID OF US.

ONCE AGAIN...

...THE DEVIL WAS ON HIS WAY.
FUTURE CONSTRUCTION SITE
MILLENNIUM DEVELOPMENTS
FOR YOUR FUTURE
FOR OUR FUTURE
KANE
CONSTRUCTION ZONE

THE NEXT DAY AT SCHOOL WAS A TOTAL CIRCUS.
ONLY CLOWNS DISCRIMINATE!
CLASS (OF) CLOWNS!
FILM CLUB
GET IT? CIRCUS? CLOWNS?
YEAH, YOU GET IT.
ANYPOODLE, IVY SAID IT WAS TIME TO GET FEMINIST.
SHE DIDN'T SAY IT EXACTLY LIKE THAT BUT YOU GET THE IDEA.
STAND UP AGAINST DISCRIMINATION! STAND UP FOR WOMEN IN FILM! STAND UP FOR DIVERSITY!
DON'T BE A CLOWN! THE FILM CLUB SUCKS MONKEYS!
IVY WAS SO SMART. SHE EVEN HAD A REASON FOR US TO DRESS UP LIKE CLOWNS. BECAUSE OF THIS GROUP CALLED THE GUERRILLA GIRLS.
ALL THE MEMBERS WEAR GORILLA MASKS AND THEY RAISE AWARENESS ABOUT HOW FEW WOMEN ARTISTS GET TO BE IN MUSEUMS AND HAVE THEIR WORK VALUED IN THE PATRIARCHY.
THAT'S WHY WE'RE CLOWNS!
YEAH, YOU KNOW. IT'S A TRIBUTE.
WHAT IF WE DRESSED LIKE THIS ALL THE TIME?!

NICE SHOES.
IT'S NOT NICE, BUTTFACE, IT'S A *PROTEST!*
I LOVE THAT YOU THINK THERE'S SOME MERIT IN PROTESTING STANLEY KUBRICK.
YOU WANT TO TALK VISUAL THEMES IN *THE SHINING*, I'M GAME, OKAY?
THAT'S NOT WHAT THIS IS ABOUT.
OH! SO IT'S ***NOT*** A PROTEST. I'M SORRY, I MUST BE CONFUSED. THIS IS JUST HOW YOU DRESS.
YOU BOOGER.
THIS IS ABOUT WHAT YOU'RE KEEPING ***OUT*** OF THE PICTURE. THIS IS A DIVERSE SCHOOL, AS A SCHOOL CLUB YOU HAVE A RESPONSIBILITY.
OH PLEASE.
IT'S NOT MY PROBLEM THAT WOMEN HAVEN'T MADE ANY DECENT FILMS.
SAYS YOU.
YES. ***AND*** I'M SAYING I DON'T HAVE TIME FOR THIS.
DON'T MESS WITH ME, MISS IVY, YOU'LL LOSE.
I'M GOING TO PANTS HIM.
FEMINIST CLOWNS DON'T PANTS. WE PLAN OUR NEXT MOVE.

IVY SAID THE GUERRILLA GIRLS WORE MASKS BECAUSE THEY WANTED PEOPLE TO FOCUS ON THE ISSUES, NOT ON THEIR FACES.
OF COURSE, PEOPLE AT THIS SCHOOL KNOW WHO WE ARE, SO IT DOESN'T WORK THE SAME WAY. BUT I LIKE THE IDEA THAT WE'RE MAKING IT ABOUT THE MESSAGE.
YEAH! YOU THINK MAYBE THEY WORE MASKS BECAUSE ALSO THERE'S STUFF YOU CAN SAY AS A CLOWN THAT YOU CAN'T SAY AS A REGULAR-TYPE PERSON?
STUFF LIKE HONK! HONK!
GOOD POINT.
ANYWAY. I DON'T KNOW IF WE SHOULD STICK WITH THIS PARTICULAR APPROACH, BUT THANKS FOR DOING THIS.
WHUT? I LOVE BEING A CLOWN! I'M NEVER EVER TAKING THIS OFF.
WELL, THAT'S... GOOD.
HEY, I HEARD ABOUT WHAT HAPPENED TO YOUR BUILDING.
YEAH. THEY TRIPLE-QUADRA-UPLED THE RENT. LIKE, SO SO MUCH.
MILLENNIUM ENTERPRISES.
THE KANES?
THE ONGOING CORPORATE TAKEOVER OF LOWER GOTHAM.

MAMA SAYS THEY'RE EVICTING THE GUYS AT GOTHAM CONVENIENCE, TOO.
THEY'RE BUILDING MORE CONDOS. AND STORES FOR PEOPLE WHO LIVE IN CONDOS, PEOPLE WHO CAN AFFORD TO LIVE WHEREVER THEY WANT AND DO WHATEVER THEY WANT.
WHO ARE HAPPY TO GET RID OF THE PEOPLE WHO CAN'T.
THAT SUCKS.
MILLENNIUM ENTERPRISES, A.K.A. KANE FOODS. KANE CONDOS. KANE COFFEE. IT'S ALL THE SAME THING. ONE GIANT COMPANY.
RICH PEOPLE AND BIG BUSINESS MOVE IN, POOR PEOPLE AND SMALL BUSINESSES GET PUSHED OUT. MY MOM SAYS THE CITY IS ALREADY WAY MORE GENTRIFIED THAN WHEN SHE WAS A KID...
I'M SORRY ABOUT MAMA. I MEAN IF HE DOESN'T OWN THE BUILDING. IT'S NOT AN EASY FIGHT.
YEAH. WELL.
MAMA SAYS LIFE IS HELL BUT...

"...THE DRAG SHOW MUST GO ON."
MAMA, BEING A FAIRY-GODPERSON TYPE, WASN'T GOING TO LET CORPORATE BOOGERS WIN WITHOUT AT LEAST **DRAGGIN'** THE WHOLE THING OUT A LITTLE.
MaMa's
HEY QUEENS! GIVE US YOUR MONEY!
FUND RAISER!
GOD SAVE YOUR LOCAL QUEENS!
SO HE GATHERED THE QUEENS TOGETHER, AND OPENED THE DOORS, AND PUT THE STAGE LIGHTS ON AND TRIED TO MAKE LOADS OF DOUGH TO SAVE THE CASTLE.
$
OKAY, YOU LUCKY, RELATIVELY GOOD-LOOKING PEOPLE!
HAND OVER YOUR DOLLAH BILLS! THIS LIFESTYLE AIN'T CHEAP, YA KNOW.
WHAT IS THAT, YOUR LUNCH MONEY? GIMME.

GIRL, UNLESS YOU WANT AN EYEFUL OF MAKEUP YOU NEED TO SIT STILL.
EH.
I REALLY HOPE WE CAN RAISE THIS MONEY. I CAN'T AFFORD A NEW PLACE.
MAMA WILL SAVE US.
HUMPH.
MAMA IS THROWING A HAIL MARY, MARY! YOU THINK WE'RE GOING TO MAKE, LIKE, EIGHT THOUSAND OR WHATEVER WE NEED? EVERY MONTH?
WHO'S MARY?
IGNORE HER.
THIS NEIGHBORHOOD IS GOING TO BE ALL SWALLOWED UP BY THE RICH, GOBBLE GOBBLE, SWEETIE PIE, AND I DON'T THINK THERE'S MUCH WE CAN DO ABOUT IT...

...'CEPT EARN THOSE DOLLAH BILLS, **HONEY!**

HEY.

DON'T LISTEN TO ***MAXIMA.*** ALL IS NOT LOST.

WE ARE ARTISTS AND CREATORS. WE MUST RELISH OUR POWER TO RESIST THE WORLD ORDER, WHICH LIES IN OUR ABILITY TO IGNORE THEIR RULES AND IMPOSE OUR OWN.

YOU LOOK LIKE A HARLEQUIN.

HARLEEN THE HARLEY QUINN.

HELLO, YOU BEAUTIFUL PEOPLE OUT THERE! HOW YOU DOING? YOU LOOK GOOD! ***YOU*** *LOOK VERY NICE. SEE ME LATER, HOT STUFF.*

I AM SO HAPPY TO HAVE YOU ALL HERE. I'M SO HAPPY, I'M EVEN WEARING MY GOOD STOCKINGS, IMAGINE THAT.
I AM MAMA AND I WANT TO WELCOME YOU TO OUR LITTLE FUNDRAISER, 'CAUSE WE NEED SOME MONEY SO WE CAN STAY HERE AND KEEP ENTERTAINING YOU.
NOW PLEASE WELCOME BACK TO THE STAGE MAXIMA IMPACT.
HEY, GUYS. YOU WANT I SHOULD SING YOU SOMETHING? YOU WANT I SHOULD SING YOU A LITTLE BLUES?
NO!
BOO!
OH. I SEE. YOU WANT SOME DISCO?
LET'S SEE WHAT MAXIMA CAN SERVE UP FOR YOU TONOIGHT.
oooOoooooo...
THERE IS SOMETHING MAGICALLY LOVELY ABOUT WATCHING PEOPLE SING.
IT'S LIKE WATCHING PEOPLE BE THEIR MOST PERSON. IT'S LIKE WATCHING THEM BE THEIR TRUE TRUE.

HARLEEN LOVED BEING SURROUNDED BY PEOPLE WHO WERE FEELING SO HAPPY. IT MADE HER FEEL GOOD AND SAFE. LIKE A BUG SNUG IN A RUG.
MAXI-MAH!
UNFORTUNATELY, THIS IS A STORY ABOUT DEVILS AND ANGELS AND NOT ABOUT DISCO AND BEING AWESOME.
CRASH
WHAT WAS THAT?

THIS IS NOT A STORY ABOUT FEELING GOOD AND SAFE.
IT'S LOTS OF THINGS, OKAY? BUT IT'S NOT THAT. IT'S ALSO NOT A STORY ABOUT GIRAFFES OR CUPCAKES. BECAUSE CUPCAKES ARE JUST LITTLE FAKE CAKES AND DO NOT DESERVE A STORY.
GO AWAY
OKAY.
SO. LET'S HIPPOTHERICALLY SAY YOU HAVE A SITUATION WHERE SOMEONE HAS DONE SOMETHING REALLY, REALLY BOOGERISH.
WHAT DO YOU DO?
DO YOU, A: JUST GO ABOUT YOUR BUSINESSES?

OR DO YOU, B: FIND THE BOOGERS RESPONSIBLE AND TAKE OUT A LITTLE WELL-DESERVED POUNDIN'?
A BUNCHA YEARS AGO.
WHEN ARE YOU GETTING THAT WRETCHED VAN OUT OF HERE?
MOM! I TOLD YOU IT'S MY FRIEND DEREK'S, OKAY? JESUS, JUST RELAX.
DO NOT TALK TO ME THAT WAY, REGGIE. I WON'T HAVE IT.
POP QUIZ, ATTENTIVE FAIRY-TALE-TIME LISTENERS, WHICH ONE DO YOU THINK WAS THE PICKED CHOICE OF LITTLE HARLEEN?
ORANGE SUGAR 100%
COME ON! NO CONTEST! AS IF LITTLE HARLEEN WAS GONNA LET SOME LOOGER BOOGER TAKE HER VAN AND LEAVE IT LIKE A WET TEDDY ON HIS FRONT LAWN.
I TOLD YOU THEY WOULDN'T CALL THE COPS. LET'S JUST TAKE THE VAN TO THE LAKE AND TORCH IT.
HEY, REGGIE.
ALSO, HOW IS REGGIE A REAL PERSON'S NAME? WHAT KIND OF STUCK-UP DORK NAMES THEIR KID REGGIE?

HOW 'BOUT YOU GET YOUR FILTHY PAWS OFF MY MOM'S VAN BEFORE I SQUASH YOU LIKE A GUMMY BEAR, YOU BOOGER!
WHAT THE--?
GET THE FRICK OFF MY PROPERTY OR I'LL CALL THE COPS, STUPID TRASH.
THERE ARE CERTAIN THINGS YOU SHOULD NEVER CALL A PERSON AND IF YOU CALL A PERSON THAT THING...
...THAT PERSON GETS TO KICK THE SNOT OUT OF YOU.
TRASH IS ONE OF THOSE THINGS.
I'M GONNA MAKE LIKE A DENTIST AND REMOVE ALL YOUR TOOTHS, YOU DIRTY, LOWDOWN--
OH MY GOD! POLICE!

SOMEONE! CALL THE POLICE!
THIS WAS NOT HARLEEN'S FIRST OFFENSE.
APPARENTLY IF YOU DO THIS ENOUGH TIMES, THEY BOOK YOU FOR REALS.
5.0
5.0
4.0
4.0
8-1-18-12-5-5-14
HARLEEN QUINZEL
PUTTHOLE POLICE DEPT.
3.0
3.0
ALSO APPARENTLY, THERE ARE SOME THINGS THAT, IF A PERSON WANTS TO DO THEM, THEY SHOULD DO ANONYMOUSLY.

MAMA CALLED HIS BAT HIS "MAGIC WAND." HE SAID IT WAS FOR BAD COMPANY.
THAT SOUNDS LIKE A PRETTY GOOD NAME FOR A BAT, DON'T YOU THINK?
DO DO DO!
BAD COMPANY.
OH, HELLO!
I ALSO THINK FRED AND ANGELA ARE GOOD BAT NAMES.
EIGHT BUCKS!
KANE COFFEE
BOHEMIAN LATTE $8
MAYBE AT THIS POINT YOU ARE THINKING, HEY, WHAT'S THE DEAL? YOU GOT SOMETHING AGAINST COFFEE?

ASK YOURSELF, SMARTY-PAJAMAS, IF IT WAS JUST SOME COCOA LATTE COINKY-DINK THAT THE KANE COFFEE PEOPLE WERE COMIN' TO TAKE MAMA'S PLACE AND THE SAME CUP SHOWED UP OUTSIDE RIGHT AFTER THE WINDOW GOT BUSTED?
THE SAME COMPANY TRYING TO TAKE OVER THE NEIGHBORHOOD AND BUILD SOME UGLY WHATSITS!
HARLEEN'S AT THE PLATE.
WHAT ARE YOU, SOME KIND OF MACAROON?
STRIKE ONE!
BOHEMI
LATTE
THESE BUSINESS BOOGERS WERE COMING FOR MAMA, AND IT WAS TIME TO SEND A MESSAGE.
SPECIAL DELIVERY-LIKE
IT'S A HOME RUN!

NOICE!
WEEP
WEEP
WEEP
UH-OH.
'COURSE IN THIS NEIGHBORHOOD, A WINDOW GETS BUSTED, COPS ARRIVE LICKETY-SPLI--
ROOOEEOOOREEOO
RUN!

HEY! WHO ARE YOU?!
RUN, RUN, LITTLE RABBIT, IF YOU DON'T WANT TO GO TO THE CLINK.
THE CLINK?
WHO SAYS THE CLINK? WHAT'RE YOU, SOME OLD-TIMEY GUY?
CLINKETY CLINK.
ISN'T THERE A STORY ABOUT A GIRL WHO WENT DOWN A RABBIT HOLE OR SOMETHING AND THEY GAVE HER CAKE AND THEN SOMEONE TRIED TO CHOP HER HEAD OFF? I THINK THERE IS.
THIS ISN'T THAT STORY EITHER BUT WHATEVER.

WHEN HARLEEN'S MOM WAS FEELING LOST, SHE'D SAY SHE WAS DOWN THE BUNNY HOLE.
WHICH IS ONLY FUNNY BECAUSE HARLEEN'S MOM WAS ALSO AFRAID OF BUNNIES. BECAUSE OF THEIR BIG, SCARY TEETH.
HARLEEN WASN'T AFRAID OF BUNNIES OR BUNNY HOLES.
NICE PLACE. MUSTY.

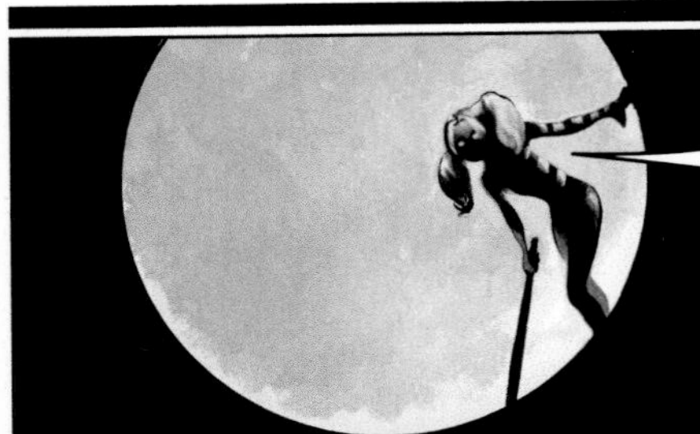

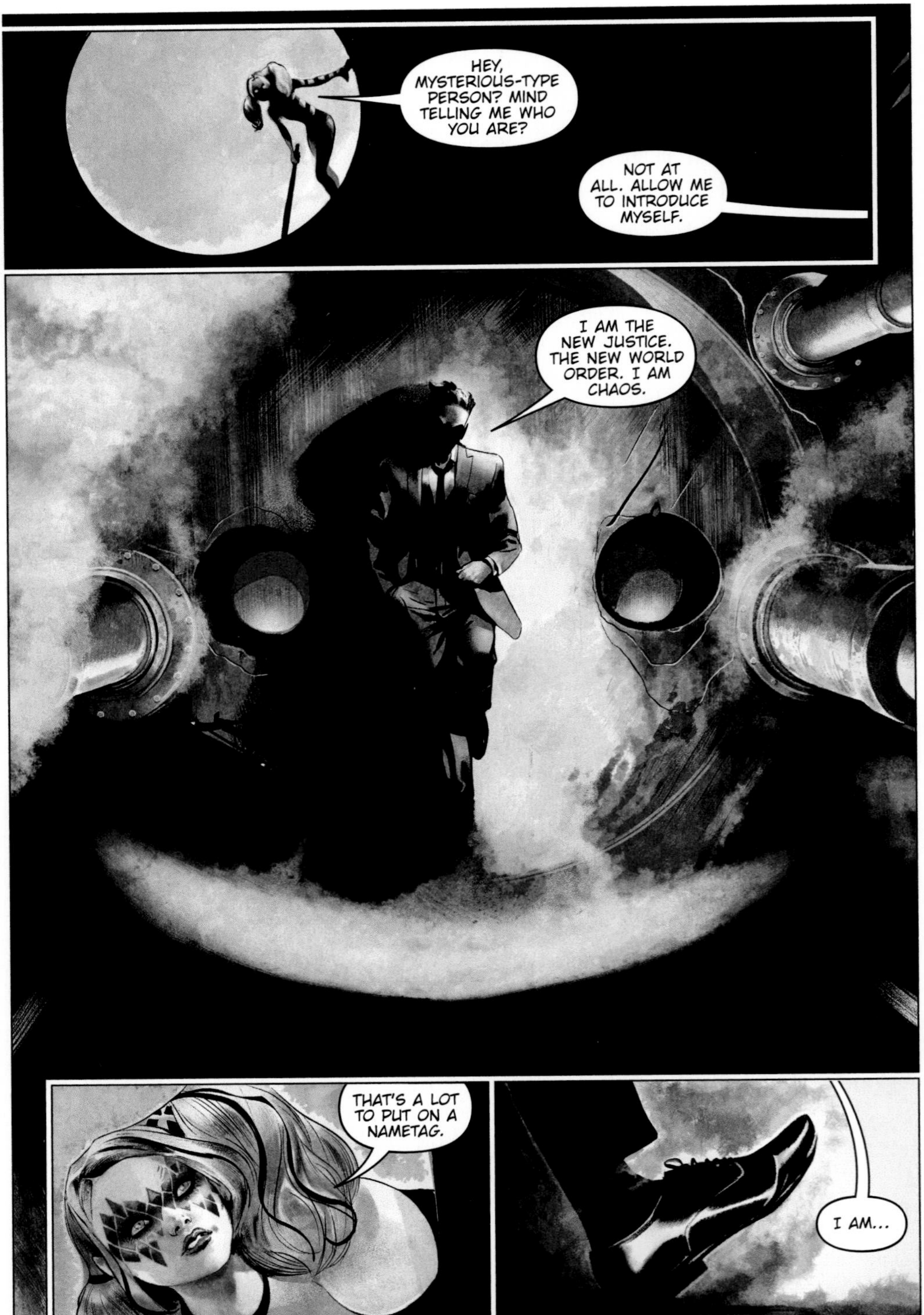

I AM THE NEW JUSTICE. THE NEW WORLD ORDER. I AM CHAOS.

...THE
JOKER.
BUT YOU
CAN CALL ME...
THE JOKER.
SORRY
I CAN'T
STAY.
EE
IT WAS
A PLEASURE
MAKING YOUR
ACQUAINTANCE.
NICE TO
MEET YOU, TOO,
BUNNY.

CHAPTER THREE

MMMMMM MMM MMM, MMM MMM MMM.
MMMMMM MMM MMM.

OVER HERE!
NOT IN THE FACE, DEBBIE!
THE NEXT DAY, OUR HERO RECAPPED TO HER NEW BEST FRIEND WHAT HAD GONE DOWN THE NIGHT BEFORE.
WHICH WAS A LOT OF STUFF.
OF COURSE, FOR SECURITY REASONS, SHE DID MAKE SOME CHANGES TO HER STORY.
YOU KNOW, IN CASE ANY FED-TYPES WERE LISTENING.
LIKE, INSTEAD OF BAT SHE SAID...
GOOD THING I HAD MY SALAMI WITH ME...
UHHHH, WHAAT?
ALL RIGHT, LADIES, THAT'S IT. HIT THE SHOWERS!

HOLD UP.
SO. FIRST. MAMA'S WINDOW WAS SMASHED.
YUP.
SECOND. YOU SMASHED A WINDOW?
YES. OKAY, BUT FIRST, IT WAS A KANE COFFEE, AND MY IDEA, WHICH I GOT FROM YOU, IS THAT KANE COFFEE IS BASICALLY IN KAZOO WITH MILLENNIUM SOUL-CRUSHERS, WHO ARE TRYIN' TO TAKE OVER MAMA'S.
OKAY. SECOND.
THIRD.
THIRD, THIS GUY WHO SAVED YOU SAID HIS NAME WAS "THE JOKER"?
LIKE, YOU'RE NOT SAYING, "THIS GUY'S A JOKER." YOU'RE SAYING HE SAID HE WAS THE JOKER.
YUP. ALSO, HE HAD A MASK ON, SO--
OKA--
OH COME ON!

EVEN MORE WHITE MEN. WHITE MEN AND DAMSELS IN DISTRESS. ALSO, SINCE WHEN IS FILM NOIR AN *EXTRAVAGANZA?* LIKE WHAT, IS THAT SOME LAME ATTEMPT TO USE THE LANGUAGE OF QUEER CULTURE TO TRY AND MAKE YOURSELF LOOK COOL?
FILM CLUB
FILM NOIR EXTRAVAGANZA
LUCKY THIRTEEN
NIGHT
ALSO. HOW COME ALL THE GUYS ON THIS POSTER ARE IN SUCH A BAD MOOD?
OKAY. BACK ON TRACK.
YES.
HOW DO YOU KNOW THIS JOKER GUY ISN'T THE ONE WHO SMASHED MAMA'S WINDOW?
OOOOOO! GOOD QUESTION!
YEAH, GOOD QUESTION. AND I'M NOT TELLING YOU WHAT TO DO, AND I HATE KANE COFFEE AND MILLENNIUM, TOO, BUT...
IN GOTHAM, AS WITH MANY OTHER PLACES, PEOPLE WITH NO MONEY...
...YOU NEED TO BE CAREFUL, HARLEEN. IF *YOU* GET CAUGHT BREAKING WINDOWS, THAT'S A CRIME.

"...GO TO JAIL FOR THAT SORT OF THING."
ARE WE GOING TO THROW SOME GLITTER ON IT OR SOMETHING? IT LOOKS A LITTLE GRIM.
TALK ABOUT ROUGH EDGES.
GIVE U. YOUR MONEY!
IT **BE** GRIM, MY LITTLE DUCKLINGS. IT **BE** GRIM.
MR. HAN-**GUSTAFSSON.**
MR. KANE, MRS. KANE. HOW CAN I HELP YOU?
I HOPE THIS ISN'T A BAD TIME.
NOT AT ALL.
LOOK AT YOU FIXING THAT UP. IT'S... FABULOUS. ISN'T THAT WHAT YOU SAY? ***FABULOUS.***
NOT ANY-MORE.
HARLEEN'S MOM COULD ALWAYS SPOT A DEVIL.

UNFORTUNATELY THE BUILDING HAS BEEN CONDEMNED, MR. HAN-GUSTAFSSON...
CONDEMNED? BUT IT JUST PASSED--
AT MILLENNIUM ENTERPRISES, WE BELIEVE IT'S TIME FOR A NEW FACE, A NEW HOPE FOR THIS CRUMBLING COMMUNITY.
SHE SAID MOST DEVILS TRY TO DISGUISE THEMSELVES.
DID YOU KNOW VIOLENCE HAS BEEN ESCALATING IN THESE NEIGHBORHOODS? YOURS ISN'T THE ONLY SMASHED WINDOW.
BUT IF YOU LOOK, YOU CAN ALWAYS SEE IT IN THEIR SMILE.
HARLEEN'S MOTHER SAID TO WATCH OUT FOR ANY-ONE WHO CAN'T SMILE WITH THEIR EYES.
HOW LONG--
OUR CONTRACTORS HAVE INFORMED US THAT IN ORDER TO STAY ON SCHEDULE...
YOU KNOW HOW THESE CONTRACTORS ARE...
I REALLY DON'T, MR. KANE.
A SMILE WITHOUT EYES IS LIKE A CARROT ON AN ICE CREAM SUNDAE.
NOTICE

IT TRULY HAS BEEN A PLEASURE DOING BUSINESS WITH YOU...UH, MR. HAN-GUSTAFSSON.
IT LEAVES A BAD TASTE IN YOUR MOUTH.
A PLEASANT AFTERNOON TO YOU ALL.
I THOUGHT WE HAD MORE TIME.
YOU WERE WRONG, MAMA.
THEY DIDN'T SAY ANYTHING ABOUT CONDEMNED. THEY SAID THEY WERE GOING TO RAISE THE RENT.
THEY LIED.
THEY LIED.

OLD QUEENS DON'T CRY, KIDDO. THEY JUST DON'T.
MaMa's
DON'T WORRY, MAMA. IT'LL BE ALL RIGHT
IT'S OKAY, MAMA.
YOU KNOW I'VE BEEN IN THIS PLACE TWENTY YEARS.
WHEN DO THEY WANT US OUT?

THAT NIGHT, MIA GOT ON STAGE AND LIP-SYNCHED ALL HER SADDEST SONGS.
EVEN THE SONGS SHE STOPPED SINGING AFTER HER STUPID EX-BOYFRIEND STOLE HER LAPTOP.
THE SONGS SHE STOPPED SINGING BECAUSE THEY WERE HIS FAVORITE SONGS AND HE WAS A PUSS HEAD.
NOT THAT HARLEEN WAS THERE TO HEAR THEM.
HEY, WHERE'S HARLEEN?
BECAUSE HARLEEN WAS OUT LOOKIN' FOR A JOKER.
DOO DOO DO DOOOO!
SHE HAD AN IDEA OF WHERE SHE COULD FIND HIM. SINCE THE JOKER SEEMED LIKE A BIT OF A MONSTER.
HELLLOOOOOO!
AND MONSTERS...
...COME OUT AT NIGHT.
WELL HELLO, STRANGER.

WHAT'S A NICE GIRL LIKE YOU DOING OUT SO LATE? ISN'T IT PAST YOUR BEDTIME?
WHUUU--
OH, YOU'RE TALKIN' TO ME!
WHAT ARE YOU, THE BEDTIME POLICE OR SOME-THING?
WHAT'RE YOU DOING?

WHO, ME?
YEAH. YOU.
I'M JUST HAVING A LITTLE FUN. YOU?
ALSO FUN.
INTERESTING. SEEMS WE HAVE SOMETHING IN COMMON.
YOU THINK SO?
I DO.
WOULD YOU LIKE TO JOIN ME FOR A LITTLE STROLL?
YEAH, OKAY.

YOU KNOW WHAT I HATE, LITTLE RABBIT?
RAINBOWS?
I HATE THINGS THAT ARE *BORING.*

YOU KNOW WHAT'S BORING, LITTLE RABBIT?
UHHH. LEMME SEE.
THE BUS?
NAH, THE BUS ISN'T BORING. THE BUS IS AWESOME.
WHAT ABOUT...REALLY SMALL PIECES OF PAPER?
EXCEPT CONFETTI IS LITTLE PIECES OF PAPER AND CONFETTI IS AWESOME SPAGHETTI SAUCE.
THIS IS KIND OF A WEIRD GAME. CAN YOU GIVE ME A HI--
THIS *CITY*.
THIS CITY IS BORING ME TO TEARS.

THIS CITY OF--
HEY, MR. TALKSALOT. I KNOW YOU WANNA TALK ABOUT WHAT'S BORING, BUT I GOTTA QUICK QUESTION. DID YOU HAPPEN TO BE GETTING SO BORED THAT YOU SMASHED MAMA'S WINDOW?
WHAT?
NOW, WHY WOULD I DO THAT?
AND SAVE YOU?
DOESN'T MAKE ANY SENSE. DOES IT?
YEAH, BUT PEOPLE DO THINGS THAT DON'T MAKE SENSE ALL THE TIME.
THEY CERTAINLY DO.
THEY CERTAINLY DO.
WHEN YOU'RE RIGHT, YOU'RE RIGHT.
SO MUCH INSIGHT, MISS...

I'M SORRY. WITH ALL MY PONTIFICATING, I DIDN'T GET YOUR NAME.
KANE COFFEE
HARL- HARLEY.
HARLEY QUINN.
HARLEY QUINN. HOW LOVELY.
WELL, HARLEY QUINN. IT'S NICE TO MAKE YOUR ACQUAINTANCE.
I DO BELIEVE THIS COULD BE THE START...
CLICK

...OF A BEAUTIFUL FRIENDSHIP.
WHOA.
KABOOM
KANE

HARLEY QUINN, YOU'VE FOUND ME AT A VERY INTERESTING POINT IN MY...EVOLUTION...
I'M SHAKING THINGS UP.
I'M SUMMONING FORTH... A REVOLUTION.
WITH A LITTLE FIRE AND BRIMSTONE.
BOOM
ROOOEEEOO REEEOOO
BEAUTIFUL, ISN'T IT?
IT'S NOT BORING.
WE WILL MEET AGAIN, HARLEY QUINN!
LUMPIN' LOLLIPOPS! THE COPS!
SO...
...MAYBE THERE'S SOMETHING I SHOULD MAKE CLEAR AT THIS POINT IN THE STORY.
KANE
ROOOEEEOOOREEEEROOOEE

IN CASE YOU'RE MISTHINKING ABOUT WHAT KIND OF STORY THIS IS.
PD
STILL.
IN CASE YOU'RE SITTIN' THERE THINKIN' MAYBE THIS HARLEEN CHARACTER IS SOMEONE SHE'S NOT.
LET ME BE CLEAR LIKE THE WATERS OF NO RIVER OR BODY OF WATER I EVER LIVED NEXT TO.

KABOOM.
YOU KNOW HOW SOME FAIRY TALES HAVE A SWEET, WIDE-EYED PRINCESS TYPE WHO HAS LONG HAIR, WEARS BIG SKIRTS, AND TALKS TO ANIMALS?
YEAH WELL, THIS STORY HAS NONE OF THAT.
THIS IS THE STORY OF HARLEEN QUINZEL.
GET READY TO JUMP BACK IN TIME AGAIN, KITTENS.

BACK WHEN HARLEEN QUINZEL WAS LITTLE HARLEEN.
DISTRICT JUVENILE COURT
AFTER SHE PUNCHED THE SNOT OUT OF REGGIE, BECAUSE SHE HAD A RECORD ALREADY, SHE HAD TO STAND UP IN FRONT OF A JUDGE WITH BIG, RED HAIR AND GLASSES AS BIG AS HER HEAD, WHO HAD A PICTURE OF A LADY BEHIND HER WITH A BIG SET OF SCALES, AND HARLEEN HAD TO SUPER-DUPER WITH ALL THE TOPPINGS SWEAR TO GOD TO BE GOOD.
HARLEEN'S MOM SAID, "PROMISE ME, ANGEL."
AND HARLEEN DID PROMISE.

SHE ALSO WONDERED WHY SHE HAD TO SWEAR TO THE HEAVEN-TYPES WHEN THE BOOGER WHO GOT HER IN TROUBLE AFTER HE STOLE HER VAN WAS OUT THERE SKIPPY-DIPPING AROUND LIKE IT'S HIS BIRTHDAY?
REGGIE. REMEMBER THIS JERK?
I DON'T EVEN GIVE A SHIT. MRS. HALPERN IS A BITCH.
YEAH.
THAT'S WHAT I'M SAYIN'.
JERK'S FRIENDS.
WHY THE HELL DO I NEED FRENCH? LIKE ANYONE'S GONNA SPEAK FRENCH IN BUSINESS.
LIKE, IT'S CALLED AMERICA, DUDE.
DON'T THINK SO.
ALL I'M GONNA DO THIS SUMMER IS STEAL CARS AND CAUSE SHIT.
SCREW ALL THAT OTHER SHIT.
HOLY SHIT!

WHAT GOOD IS BEING AN ANGEL WHEN YOUR MOM LOST HER JOB AT THE RESTAURANT SHE WORKED AT BECAUSE REGGIE'S DAD WAS GOLFING BRUHS WITH THE BRUH WHO OWNED BURGER EXPRESS?
HEY, REGGIE-KINS.
DID REGGIE CARE THAT HARLEEN'S MOM USED TO WORK THE FRYER AND HER HAIR ALWAYS SMELLED LIKE FRENCH FRIES? LIKE FRENCH FRIES AND HAIR SPRAY AND FRENCH FRIES IN A FRENCH-FRY-AND-HAIR-SPRAY SANDWICH?
NICE BIKES.
PROB NOT.
HEY, UH, JUST. PLEASE. DON'T--
GASOLINE
ANGELS AND DEVILS.
YOU KNOW WHO CARES ABOUT ANGELS AND DEVILS?

NOT DEVILS.
ALSO.
KNOW WHAT'S SWEETER THAN THE SMELL OF KEROSENE, AND THE SWEET, SWEET SMELL OF REVENGE?
ME NEITHER.
YOU TELL YOUR MOM ABOUT THIS, I'M GONNA BLOW UP YOUR FANCY LITTLE HOUSE IN THE 'BURBS, BUTTFACE.

WHO THE HELL WAS THAT?!
HOLY SHIT!
UH.
NO ONE...
LA LA LA! BURNING! LA LA LA LA LA! BUTTAFACE. LA LA LA!

GOOD THING HARLEEN LIVED WITH PEOPLE WHO DIDN'T THINK IT WAS WEIRD TO GO OUT LATE ALL DRESSED UP.
PIZZA!
YOU MISSED MY SONG. I SANG "THE WAY WE WERE."
HEY! YOU IN THE QUINN FULL-TIME NOW?
THINKIN' ABOUT IT.
WHERE'S MAMA?
UM. I THINK MAMA'S TAKING A NAP.
HE'S IN HIS ROOM.
IS HE OKAY?
YOU DON'T KNOW MAMA THAT WELL, HQ. HE'S SURVIVED MORE THINGS THAN ANYONE ELSE I KNOW. HE HAS SURVIVED THE *ICE AGE.*
WHAT DOES THAT MEAN?
IT MEANS HE'S TIRED, HQ. REALLY TIRED.
WE'RE ALL TIRED.

CREEEE
MAMA? ARE YOU OKAY?

CHAPTER FOUR

GNN
LIVE
...A TRIO OF MYSTERIOUS FIRES IN THE CITY TONIGHT...
...WITH DOWNTOWN GOTHAM STORES TARGETED...
...IN WHAT POLICE ARE DESCRIBING AS AN UNPRECEDENTED "HOOLIGAN SPREE."

THE CLOSEST SCHOOL COMES TO TALKING ABOUT ANGELS AND DEVILS IS SOMETHING CALLED SOCIAL SCIENCES, BUT IT IS ULTRA-MEGA-BORING.
Summarize and explain using an example of one of the conflicts we have studied in class: Those who do not study history are doomed to repeat it.*
*based on the work of philos
George Santayana
WHAT?
DOOM!
MISS QUINZEL! KEEP YOUR EYES ON YOUR PAPER!

THOSE WHO DON'T KNOW THEIR HISTORY ARE **DOOMED** TO REPEAT IT.
WHAT THE HELL. HE'S CALLING HIMSELF **GANGSTER** NOW?
STILL GANGSTERS
BOQUAHHAAAA!
WHAT'RE YOU DOING NOW?
I'M GOING TO THE COMMUNITY GARDEN... YOU CAN COME IF YOU WANT.
WHEN HARLEEN WAS A LITTLE KID, HER PARENTS ALWAYS LIVED IN PLACES WHERE THERE WEREN'T A LOT OF OTHER KIDS.
FOR A LONG TIME, HARLEEN'S BEST FRIEND WAS MABEL, WHO WAS 82 AND HAD A MAGICAL STORMY EYE AND WAS ALWAYS SAYING STUFF LIKE, "WELL, THAT'S WHAT YOU THINK."
PROPERTY PURCHASED BY
MILLENIUM DEVELOPMENTS
FOR YOUR FUTURE
FOR OUR FUTURE
CLOSED
WE BUY HOUSES

IVY WAS NOT LIKE THAT AT ALL.
FOR ONE THING, IVY SMELLED LIKE PLANTS, NOT SOUP AND CATS.
GARDE
COMMUN
OUR Community Garden
...YEAH. WELL, WE SAW IT COMING.
HEY, SWEETIE.
HEY, DAD.
I'M JUST GOING TO CHECK IN ON THE TOMATOES.

MY PARENTS MET HERE. THEY STARTED THIS GARDEN WITH A LOCAL COMMUNITY CENTER.
IVY WAS THE FIRST FRIEND HARLEEN HAD EVER HAD WHO WAS SMARTER THAN SCHOOL.
ALL THE LOCALS HAVE THEIR OWN PLOTS AND WE ALL TAKE TURNS HELPING OUT.
PLANTS WERE SOME OF THE MANY THINGS IVY KNEW A LOT ABOUT.
IVY TOLD HARLEEN ONCE THAT PLANTS WERE BETTER THAN PEOPLE BECAUSE THEY MOSTLY ONLY EVER TOOK WHAT THEY NEEDED.
HARLEEN WONDERED IF PLANTS THINK PEOPLE ARE JERKS.
HEY THERE.
HEY, IVY! LOOK!

DUN DUN DUN!
I'M DEAD BECAUSE I DON'T KNOW HISTORY.
FIRST OF ALL, YOU'RE NOT SUPPOSED TO PICK THE FLOWERS.
OH. SORRY.
SECOND OF ALL, IT'S DOOMED NOT DEAD.
THIRD OF ALL, WHY DO YOU FIND THAT STATEMENT SO WEIRD?
I DUNNO. IT'S LIKE, OH, SO IF YOU DON'T READ BOOKS YOU'RE DOOMED? LIKE HISTORY IS THAT IMPORTANT?
HEY. WHAT'S WRONG?

MY FAMILY IS BEING EVICTED. THE WHOLE BLOCK IS **CONDEMNED.** WHICH MY MOM SAYS IS A TOTAL SCAM. THERE'S NO WAY THE CITY INSPECTORS WOULD COME TOGETHER LIKE THAT UNLESS SOMEONE WAS PAYING THEM OFF.
THEY'RE COMING AFTER THE COMMUNITY GARDEN. ALL THE STORES. EVERYTHING. EVERYONE I LOVE IS GOING TO LOSE THEIR HOME.
THIS IS NOT JUST ABOUT MAMA. OR YOU. OR ME.
IT'S NOT JUST ABOUT GOTHAM.
IT'S EVERYWHERE. IT'S CORPORATIONS BEFORE COMMUNITIES.
IT'S A SYSTEM THAT PROTECTS THE RICH, FUCKS THE POOR. THAT KEEPS THE POWERFUL, POWERFUL AND THE OPPRESSED, OPPRESSED.
IT ALWAYS HAS, IT ALWAYS WILL.

AND I'M SICK OF IT!

UM.
I DIDN'T... I JUST DIDN'T KNOW... ABOUT HISTORY.
LOOK...THIS GARDEN IS KIND OF LIKE MY WORLD. AND THE THOUGHT OF LOSING IT...RIGHT NOW, I JUST CAN'T...

I'M SORRY.
IVY!
I GOTTA GO. I TOLD MY DAD I WOULD WATCH THE STORE.
I WILL SAVE YOUR GARDEN, IVY.
OKAY. THANKS.
I WILL.

NOTICE!
THIS PROPERTY HAS BEEN
CONDEMNE
DOOM.
OUR HERO HARLEEN DIDN'T WANT TO MAKE IVY MAD(DER) BUT THERE WAS SOMETHING ABOUT ALL THIS THAT DIDN'T MAKE SENSE.
THIS PROPERTY IS
CONDEMNED
LIKE, IF SOMEONE'S TAKING YOUR HOUSE, WHAT ARE YOU SUPPOSED TO DO, LIKE, GO UP TO THEM AND ASK THEM IF THEY STUDIED HISTORY?
HOW DOES THAT HELP?
HEY.

IT'S JUST A LITTLE PLUMP-UP. IT'S MY BIRTHDAY PRESENT.
GIRL, YOU DO NOT WANT TO START PUTTING THAT CRAP IN YOUR FACE.
AS OPPOSED TO JUST ALL THE SHIT YOU PUT ON YOUR FACE.
THAT SHIT IS EXPENSIVE.
THEN HOW CAN YOU AFFORD IT?
IT IS PAID FOR BY MY NEW MAN, WHO WORKS AT THE COSMETICS COUNTER AT MARCY'S AND GIVES ME HIS DISCOUNT. THAT'S HOW.
HEY!
OH LOOK, IT'S THE DIVA HARLEY QUINN, EVERYONE!
THAT'S ME!

OH CRAP, SPEAKING OF, I GOTTA GO OUT AND BUY ME SOME BUTT AND MASCARA.
YOU WANNA COME BUY SOME BUTT WITH ME?
DO I?
LET'S GO!!

VALUE OF THE DOLLAR$
MISS HARLEY QUINN.
WELCOME TO THE TEMPLE OF ALL THAT IS GOOD AND COSTS A DOLLAR.
THIS PLACE IS AWESOME.
THAT PLASTIC SMELL. SOOOOOOO GOOD.
ENTIRELY POSSIBLE THAT I ONLY WENT INTO DRAG BECAUSE I'M NATURALLY TACKY.
IS THERE A BUTT SECTION?
TO ARTS AND CRAFTS, WHERE ALL GREAT THINGS ARE FOUND.
YOU THINK I CAN MAKE THIS INTO A WHOLE OUTFIT?
PRETTY!

I COULD DO A WHOLE COLLECTION OF DOLLAR-STORE COUTURE. LIKE, STREAMER BIKINIS, YOU KNOW? SOME FLIP-FLOP HATS, LIKE, PRISCILLA-STYLE.
CAN YOU MAKE ME A FLIP-FLOP BIKINI?

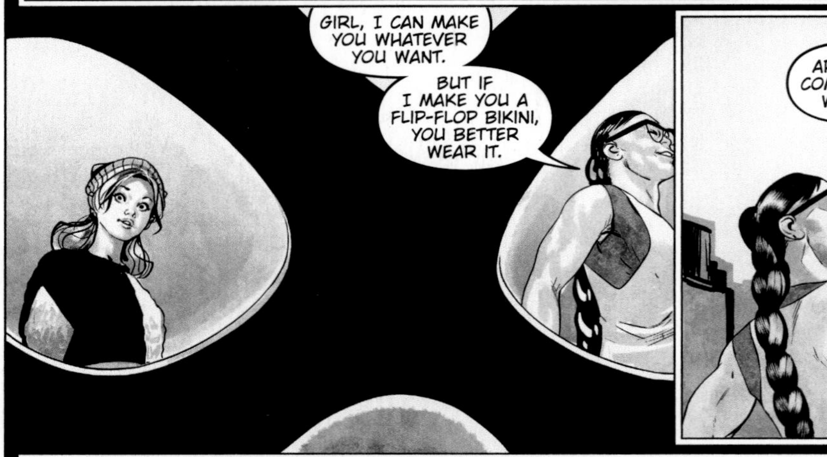
GIRL, I CAN MAKE YOU WHATEVER YOU WANT.
BUT IF I MAKE YOU A FLIP-FLOP BIKINI, YOU BETTER WEAR IT.

ARE YOU COMING OR WHAT?

HEY!

DALI, YOU GOT A DOLLAR I CAN BORROW?

I CAN'T BELIEVE YOU GOT ME SPENDING MY TIPS ON ICE CREAM!
AND THIS MASK! IT'S SO, LIKE, PARIS IS BURNING, O-PER-A REALNESS.
"WE ARE HEAH FOR THE AH-PER-AH. FOR THE DEE-VA!"
YES, WE ARE FIERCE AND WE QUEENS WILL SURVIVE FIERCELY, YES WE WILL.
EXCUSE ME.

I DON'T THINK THAT KIND OF BEHAVIOR IS APPROPRIATE IN A FAMILY ESTABLISHMENT.
EXCUSE ME.
DO NOT COME IN HERE WITH YOUR BUSTED BETTY RUBBLE YUPPIE-ASS PEARLS AND YOUR CHILDREN OF THE CORN AND TELL ME THAT I AM NOT APPROPRIATE.
THIS IS MY NEIGHBORHOOD, I'VE LIVED HERE ALL MY LIFE, YOU ARE NEW HERE. I AM A QUEEN AND I AM ENJOYING A CHOCOLATE SUNDAE AND TALKING ABOUT THE FINE ART OF BEING FIERCE, WHICH MAYBE YOU SHOULD LEARN SOMETHING ABOUT.
ALSO...

...WELCOME TO THE NEIGHBOR-HOOD.
GOOD DAY.
YEAH, BUNION FACE.
YOINK!

GOD, THESE PEOPLE! THIS NEIGHBORHOOD REALLY IS LOST.
THAT WAS AMAZING.
YOU CAN'T BE GAY WHILE MY KIDS ARE EATING ICE CREAM!
GOD, IT MAKES ME THINK OF THIS TIME THESE STRAIGHT PEOPLE CAME TO THE BAR BECAUSE THEY THOUGHT IT WAS KARAOKE AND MAMA--
DALI.
CRAP.
A SIGN IN A STORY IS NEVER A GOOD THING. A SIGN IN A STORY IS ALWAYS, LIKE, "BEWARE" OR "KEEP OFF THE LAWN."

TA-DA! A SIGN.
ALSO, YUCK.
FUTURE CONSTRUCTION SITE
MILLENNIUM DEVELOPMENTS
WE ARE THE FUTURE
SCHOOL
CONDEMNED
DO NOT ENTER

CHAPTER FIVE

DID YOU DO YOUR SPANISH HOMEWORK?
SÍ, PORQUE SOY AWESOME-SAUCE.
IT WOULD BE NICE IF THERE WERE A SIGN IN A STORY THAT JUST SAID, "FREE CANDY."
YOU KNOW WHAT ELSE WOULD BE HANDY IN A STORY? A GLASS SLIPPER. A GLASS SLIPPER IS A NICE THING TO HAVE IF YOU HAVE A STRANGER AND YOU DON'T KNOW WHO HE IS AND YOU WANT TO FIND OUT.
DO YOU THINK THE JOKER GOES TO GOTHAM HIGH?
HE SOUNDS LIKE A CLOWN TO ME.
SO MAYBE HE DOES GO TO THIS SCHOOL.
A STRANGER, A.K.A. THE JOKER, WHOM HARLEEN HAD NOT SEEN FOR A FEW DAYS.
AT THIS POINT, HARLEEN WAS 99.9999999 PERCENT SURE THE JOKER WENT TO GOTHAM, BUT HE WAS HARD TO SPOT WITH THE WHOLE MASK THING.
ALL THE GUYS WHO GO TO THIS SCHOOL ARE BOOGERS.
TRUE.

HEY, WHAT MAKES YOU THINK THE JOKER ISN'T A BOOGER?
GUH, YOU'VE GOT ME SAYING "BOOGER" NOW.
A BOOGER IS A VERY SPECIFIC PHENOMENAL.
EXACTLY.
PHENOMENON.
UM. HI. CAN WE TALK TO YOU ABOUT THE, UH, FILM CLUB?
WHEN'S YOUR NEXT PROTEST?
YES! MORE CLOWNS!
OH. UH. SOON.
WE ASKED JOHN KANE ABOUT SHOWING BOLLYWOOD MOVIES AND HE TOLD US TO GO ELSEWHERE.
WE COULD PROTEST THE NEXT SCREENING...
DO YOU GUYS WANT TO BE CLOWNS?
DO WE HAVE T--
YES!

I GOTTA GO TO MY LOCK-UP. LATER!
LOCKER.
I WAS THINKING MAYBE SPACE CLOWNS?
HERE'S A RIDDLE FOR YOU.
HOW DO YOU FIND A MYSTERIOUS STRANGER?
HE FINDS YOU.
MAYBE NOT A RIDDLE.
HEY!
BEGAAH!
WATCH YOUR STEP.
WATCH YOUR FACE!

STUPID BOOGERS.
SLAM
HOW ABOUT THEM COOKIES?
A GLASS SLIPPER.

WHY DOES MY WIG SMELL LIKE CHEETOS?
AND OTHER GREAT MYSTERIES.
For Miss Quinn. Meet me at Chickin Lickin. Midnight. -J
WHERE'S MAMA?
AMERICA'S new model
RESTING.
SOMETIMES A GLASS SLIPPER IS A GLASS SLIPPER AND SOMETIMES IT'S AN INVITATION TO A CHICKEN PLACE.
WHERE ARE YOU GOING?
CHICKEN.
BESIDES, WHO WEARS GLASS SLIPPERS THESE DAYS?
OKAY, EXCEPT FOR DRAG QUEENS?
IT'S ELEVEN THIRTY!
GET US CHICKEN!
OKAY!

THERE'S SOMETHING KINDA PEACEFUL ABOUT AN ABANDONED CHICKEN PLACE AT MIDNIGHT.
THAT SWEET SMELL OF OLD CHICKEN AND OLD PEOPLE WHO EAT CHICKEN.

A MASK. HOW ORIGINAL.
YEAH, I COULD SAY THE SAME TO YOU, MISTER.

SO, WHAT DO YOU WANT, JOKER FACE?

GETTING RIGHT TO THE POINT, I LIKE IT.

I'M HERE TO MAKE YOU AN OFFER, SO TO SPEAK.

IS IT A LIFETIME SUPPLY OF CHOCOLATE PEANUT BUTTER BARS?

NO.

A SET OF REALLY BIG PURPLE SHOES?

NO.

GUM?

NO!

I'M GOING TO TAKE DOWN KANE ENTERPRISES...

...BY CUTTING OFF ITS BIG, SWOLLEN HEAD.

I THINK IT'S SOMETHING YOU WOULD ENJOY. ISN'T IT TIME TO MAKE THE FAT CORPORATE SUITS SQUIRM? MAKE THEM PAY FOR THEIR GREED?
FOR MAMA?
THINK ABOUT IT.
THEN WHAT?
WE'LL BE IN TOUCH.

HARLEEN'S MOM USED TO LIKE THIS POEM THIS GUY WROTE ABOUT BEING AT A PLACE WHERE THERE ARE TWO ROADS AND A HORSE.
TWO ROADS AND A HORSE WALK INTO A BAR.
OtherChicke
CLOSED
SPOILER ALERT. HORSES DON'T DRINK.
OKAY, THAT'S NOT THE POEM.
OtherChic
THE POEM IS ABOUT ROADS, BUT IT DOESN'T REALLY TELL YOU ANYTHING ABOUT HOW TO PICK A ROAD. IT'S JUST LIKE, THIS IS THE ROAD THIS GUY PICKED...
OH MY GOD, I CAN ALREADY FEEL THE GREASE IN MY FACE.
OtherChicken

CHAPTER SIX

IS THAT WHY SO MANY PEOPLE DON'T LIKE POETRY? BUT EVERYONE LIKES CHICKEN?
BUT WHAT DOES IT MEAN? CAN ANYONE TALK TO ME ABOUT HOW THIS CONNECTS TO FORESHADOWING?
WHAT'S UP WITH YOU TODAY?
YOU'RE VERY QUIET FOR YOU.
WHATZA?
IT'S HARD TO THINK AND TALK AT THE SAME TIME, THAT'S ALL.
WHAT ARE YOU THINKING ABOUT?
HISTORY.
REALLY?

LIKE HOW PEOPLE CHANGE HISTORY AND WHAT YOU SAID ABOUT US BEING DOOMED AND STUFF.
NOT EXACTLY WHAT I SAID, BUT IT'S TRUE THAT YOU CAN'T CHANGE HISTORY. YOU CHANGE THE FUTURE.
I JUST MEANT, LIKE, HOW DO YOU MAKE IT BETTER, WITH HISTORY?
YOU CAN **ACKNOWLEDGE** THAT HISTORY, TO START.
DO YOU THINK THIS PROTEST IS GOING TO CHANGE THE FUTURE OF THE SCHOOL?
THE ***FUTURE*** OF THE SCHOOL? MAYBE. A ***PART*** OF IT, YEAH.
I HOPE PEOPLE WILL SEE THIS AND KNOW THE FILM CLUB MEMBERS ARE DINKS.
I THINK IT'S A STATEMENT ABOUT PREJUDICE IN THIS SCHOOL.
YEAH! LET'S DO THIS!

2001
FILM CLUB
GOOD AFTERNOON!
I WANT TO TAKE A MOMENT TO ACKNOWLEDGE THE GREAT WORK WE ARE ABOUT TO WITNESS, AND WHAT IT MEANS TO APPRECIATE THIS WORK.
EXIT
HONK! HONK!!!
THIS AFTERNOON WE SCHOLARS, WE VISIONARIES, WE REBELS, WE MAVERICKS, PAY TRIBUTE TO THE MEN WHO LIGHT THE WA--
IT'S A PROTEST, YOU BOOGERS!
WHAT UP, SPORTS FANS?!

WE STUDENTS OF THIS SCHOOL, WE ARTISTS, WE VISIONARIES, WE TRUE REBELS DEMAND TO BE HEARD!
THIS IS OUR FILM CLUB, TOO!
MOTHER LAND!
YOU BOOGERS SUCK!
HONK! HONK!
HEY! HEY!

HO! HO!
YOU GUYS ARE REAL JERK-BUTTS!
SHOW STUFF MADE BY WOMEN!
PIGS!
MI VIDA LOCA!
FRIDA!
HEY HEY!
HO! HO!
STUDENTS!

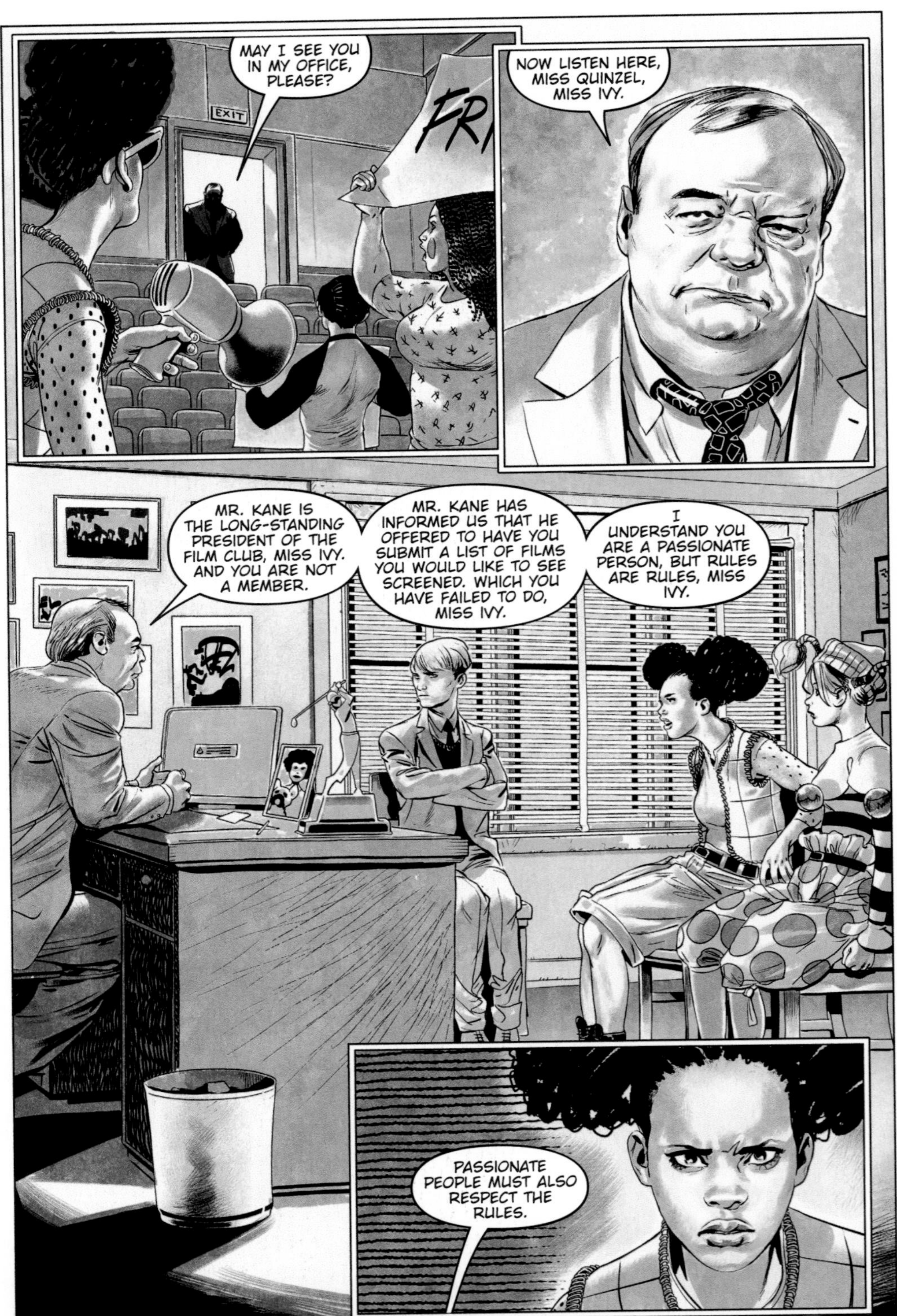
MAY I SEE YOU IN MY OFFICE, PLEASE?
EXIT
NOW LISTEN HERE, MISS QUINZEL, MISS IVY.
MR. KANE IS THE LONG-STANDING PRESIDENT OF THE FILM CLUB, MISS IVY. AND YOU ARE NOT A MEMBER.
MR. KANE HAS INFORMED US THAT HE OFFERED TO HAVE YOU SUBMIT A LIST OF FILMS YOU WOULD LIKE TO SEE SCREENED. WHICH YOU HAVE FAILED TO DO, MISS IVY.
I UNDERSTAND YOU ARE A PASSIONATE PERSON, BUT RULES ARE RULES, MISS IVY.
PASSIONATE PEOPLE MUST ALSO RESPECT THE RULES.

OF COURSE, PRINCIPAL RIVERS, THE FILM CLUB VALUES ALL INPUT.
AND THE OFFER FOR YOU TO SUBMIT YOUR IDEAS, MISS IVY, STILL STANDS.
MAY I GET BACK? THE SCREENING HAS ALREADY BEEN DELAYED.
OF COURSE, MR. KANE.
MISS IVY. DO YOU HAVE ANYTHING TO SAY?
I RESPECTFULLY SUBMIT, PRINCIPAL RIVERS, THAT PROTEST IS A LEGITIMATE FORM OF EXPRESSION. WE ARE POINTING TO THE LARGER ISSUES--
MISS IVY--
PRINCIPAL RIVERS, IF I MAY, IF YOU ARE GOING TO REFER TO JOHN KANE AS MR. KANE, AND HARLEEN AS MISS QUINZEL, THEN YOU CAN REFER TO ME AS MISS DU-BARRY.
MISS IVY, AS A STUDENT AT THIS SCHOOL, I WILL ASK YOU TO SPEAK TO ME IN A TONE THAT IS RESPECTFUL.
SO, DO WE GET TO PICK THE MOVIES NOW?
NOPE.

NO ONE MOVE. YOU GOT 'TIL FOUR P.M. THIS IS DETENTION SO ACT LIKE YOU'RE IN TROUBLE...BECAUSE YOU ARE.
DETENTIO
IT DIDN'T WORK.
IT DIDN'T WORK.
BECAUSE "MR. KANE" PAYS THE SCREENING FEES FOR THE MOVIES.
SO IT WAS NEVER GOING TO WORK?
WHAT DID YOU THINK "WORKING" WOULD LOOK LIKE?
WE GET TO SEE THE MOVIES WE WANT!
THEN WHAT WAS THE POINT?
IT DOESN'T ALWAYS WORK OUT THAT WAY.

YOU WANT JUSTICE SO BAD?
HOW ABOUT HOW PRINCIPAL RIVERS WAS A RACIST JERK TO ME...
...AND YOU JUST SAT THERE AND LET HIM "MISS IVY" ME. LIKE I WAS SOME HOUSEMAID FROM THE '50s OR SOMETHING.
WHAT?
WHAT WAS I SUPPOSED TO SAY?
HARLEEN, YOU'RE MISS QUINZEL. HE'S MR. KANE. I'M MISS IVY?
JUST... STAND UP FOR ME!
YOU WANT CHANGE, YOU GOTTA MAKE CHANGE, YOU HAVE TO *BE* CHANGE.

SHIT, MAN. SHUT UP ALREADY.
JUST TALK, TALK, TALK.
IT'S FRICKING DETENTION, MAN.
YOU KNOW, LIKE, BE DETAINED--
--HEY WHERE YOU GOIN'?

CHAPTER SEVEN

THAT NIGHT WAS ANOTHER SAD SONG NIGHT AT MAMA'S.
IT WAS SAD WITH A SIDE ORDER OF REALLY SAD.
It never rains ... SAD SONG NIGHT
MaMa's
NOTICE OF EVICTION
MIA SANG A SELENA SONG. SHE SAID IT WAS THE SADDEST SELENA SONG.
THEN MAXIMA SANG A SONG THAT WAS REALLY REALLY SAD BY CYNDI LAUPER.
THIS IS SO, SO, SO SAD!
YOU SAID IT, KIDDO.
CLAP! CLAP!
CLAP!
WHAT'S SHE SINGING?
I DON'T KNOW.

YOU ALL HAVE BEEN SO WONDERFUL, AND IT HAS BEEN MY GREAT PRIVILEGE TO BE ABLE TO PERFORM FOR YOU OVER ALL THESE YEARS.
THERE ARE A LOT OF FACES THAT AREN'T HERE, SOME FRIENDS OF MINE DIDN'T MAKE IT TO TODAY, AND TONIGHT I'M GOING TO SING A LITTLE SOMETHING I THINK THEY WOULD LIKE.

WE LOVE YOU, MAMA!

IT'S AMAZING HOW EVEN THOUGH DRAG QUEENS ARE ONLY PRETEND SINGING, IT FEELS LIKE THEY ARE REALLY SINGING.

MAMA SANG A SONG CALLED "HAPPY DAYS ARE HERE AGAIN," BUT SHE SANG IT LIKE HAPPY DAYS ARE GONE.
LIKE THAT SHOULD BE THE SONG'S NAME.

IT WAS MAKING HARLEY'S HEART BREAK INTO LITTLE ITTY-BITTY PIECES, LIKE A BROKEN COOKIE IN YOUR CHEST AND IT'S YOUR HEART.

THAT NIGHT HARLEEN WANTED TO STAY, BUT MAMA SAID A BAR'S NO PLACE FOR A KIDDO WHO HAS SCHOOL THE NEXT DAY.
HARLEEN WASN'T SURE SHE WANTED TO GO BACK TO SCHOOL.
FRAGILE
SHOES
IF MAMA DIDN'T HAVE A PLACE TO LIVE, THEN HARLEEN DIDN'T HAVE A PLACE TO LIVE.
WHICH WOULD PROBABLY MEAN HITTING THE ROAD.
NO MORE MAMA, NO MORE QUEENS, NO MORE CASTLE.
PLUS, MAYBE NOW IVY DIDN'T WANT TO BE HARLEEN'S FRIEND.
BECAUSE HARLEEN DIDN'T STAND UP FOR HER.
YOU CAN'T TAKE BACK HISTORY.

BASICALLY, EVERYTHING WAS BAD. LIKE OLD MAYONNAISE.
NICE NIGHT.
WHAT ARE YOU DOING HERE?
LOOKING FOR YOU.
AND SO, HERE I AM.
YOU SEEM DOWN IN THE DUMPS, DESPONDENT.
YOU SEEM LIKE YOU WANT TO SAY THINGS A MILLION DIFFERENT WAYS WITH A LOTTA EXTRA.

I'M A MAN OF MANY WORDS, WHAT CAN I SAY?
I'M A POET.
AND YOU KNOW IT.
INDEED.
SO, WHAT HAS YOU DOWN, MISS QUINN?
I'M TRYING TO THINK WHAT I'M SUPPOSED TO DO NEXT.
AH-HA!
WELL, WHAT DO YOU WANT TO DO?
I WANT TO HELP PEOPLE.
AH. HELPING.
THE RIGHT WAY.
WHAT'S RIGHT AND WHAT'S WRONG REALLY DEPENDS ON THE WHO, DOESN'T IT? WHAT'S RIGHT FOR PROFIT IS WRONG FOR YOUR FRIENDS. LAWS PRETEND RIGHT IS ONE THING. BUT LAWS ARE JUST AN IDEA. ONE MAN'S NOTION OF RIGHT, WHICH MIGHT NOT BE YOURS.
IT'S ALL VERY BLAH, BLAH, BLAH.

KNOW WHAT?
OH, I GET TO TALK NOW? GEEZ.
I SAY FORGET RIGHT AND WRONG.
I JUST WANT TO BE THE PERSON WHO MAKES THE MOST NOISE.
I WANT PEOPLE TO LOOK UP AND TAKE NOTICE. I WANT PEOPLE TO REMEMBER WHAT IT IS I HAVE TO SAY ABOUT THIS WORLD.
AND HOW ARE YOU GOING TO DO THAT?
WITH YOUR HELP.
I THINK YOU'RE UP FOR A LITTLE CHAOS.
ISN'T THAT MORE FUN THAN RIGHT AND WRONG?
"TOMORROW NIGHT, WE'RE GOING TO TAKE DOWN KANE TOWER. ERASE THE DATA FROM THEIR SERVERS. DATA ON ALL THE MAMAS AND THE PAPAS. AND WE'LL UPLOAD ALL THEIR SNEAKY LITTLE SECRETS TO THE MEDIA."
YOU KNOW HOW?
OF COURSE. AND CHERRY ON SUNDAE, WE BLOW UP THEIR FANCY NEW SIGN.

WHY DO YOU NEED ME?
WE NEED A GIRL, TO GET US IN THE DOOR.
WHAT DOES BEING A GIRL HAVE TO DO WITH GETTING IN A DOOR? IS IT A GIRL DOOR?
DOES IT HAVE BOOBS?
LET'S ACCEPT, SHALL WE, THE WAY OF THE REAL WORLD AND CONCUR THAT IT IS NOT OUT OF THE REALM OF POSSIBILITY THAT A SWEET LITTLE GIRL WILL HAVE MORE SWAY WITH A BUNCH OF SECURITY MEN THAN A MASKED MAN LIKE ME.
I GOTTA THINK ABOUT IT.
NOT MUCH TIME, IS THERE?
MY WAY, MAMA KEEPS HER HOUSE, AND YOU GET TO CAUSE A LITTLE CHAOS!
SOME SAY THE WORLD WILL END IN FIRE, SOME SAY IN ICE.
I THINK YOU'D LIKE A LITTLE FIRE...

CHAPTER EiGHT

BEEP BEEP BEEP!
07:24
"...I THINK YOU WANT TO MAKE SOME NOISE."
IT'S HARD TO SLEEP WHEN YOU'RE IN THE MIDDLE OF THE REALLY INTENSE PART OF YOUR FAIRY TALE.
I BET CINDERELLA NEVER SLEPT. SLEEPING BEAUTY ONLY SLEPT BECAUSE SHE WAS DRUGGED. SOME SEVEN-DWARF DRUG.
IT'S HARD TO TALK ABOUT YOUR BIG THING WHEN EVERYONE IS DEALING WITH THEIR BIG STUFF.
HEY, MAMA.
HEY, KIDDO.
A WHOLE LIFETIME OF STUFF.
SOME OF THIS IS JAMES'.
WHO'S JAMES?
HE WAS MY ONE TRUE LOVE, MY KNIGHT IN SILVER COWBOY BOOTS. HE WAS THE ORIGINAL TENANT HERE. I MOVED IN ON HIM IN SO MANY WAYS.

-SIGH- ALL THIS MISSING.
I'M ONE OF THOSE OLD, MOPING QUEENS NOW.
YOU'RE NOT MOPING! YOU'RE JUST MISSING!
MAYBE.
YOU GOING TO SCHOOL?
OH, UH. YUP.
WHEN YOU GET BACK, KIDDO, WE NEED TO TALK.
BYE, MAMA.
HAVE A GOOD DAY, KIDDO.
THAT WAS A LIE. THE GOING-TO-SCHOOL THING.
JUST A BUTTON-SIZED ONE.
'CUZ THIS IS NOT THE PART OF THE STORY WHERE THE HERO GOES TO SCHOOL TO GET HER SPANISH TEST BACK.
SOMETIMES WHEN YOU'RE NOT SURE WHAT TO DO, YOU NEED TO GO TO A PLACE THAT YOU KNOW WILL ALWAYS BE THERE FOR YOU NO MATTER WHAT.
PROPERTY PURCHASED BY:
MILLENNIUM DEVELOPMENTS
FOR YOUR FUTURE
FOR OUR FUTURE

MARKET
NOT THIS PLACE.
THIS PLACE. THE MAGICAL HOME... OF CEREAL.
HELLO, LOVELIES!
NO MATTER WHAT HAPPENS IN THE WORLD, THERE WILL ALWAYS BE HAPPY CEREAL.
HARLEY HAD TO THINK.
BUT SOMETIMES THINKING IS HARDER THAN IT LOOKS.
COME ON, CEREAL. ANY IDEAS?
NOPE!
"MOM..."

...WHAT'S THE DIFFERENCE BETWEEN THE PATH OF THE ANGELS AND THE PATH OF THE DEVIL?
TELL ME AGAIN!
HARLEEN QUINZEL, I HAVE TOLD YOU THIS MANY TIMES.
THE PATH OF THE ANGELS IS LONG AND HARD. SO HARD THAT MOST PEOPLE DON'T WANT TO TAKE IT.
THE PATH OF THE DEVIL IS A STRAIGHT-DOWN DROP.
FAST AND EASY. STRAIGHT TO HELL.
BUT HOW DO YOU **KNOW** IF YOU'RE GOING UP OR DOWN IF YOU'RE IN THE MIDDLE?
YOU KEEP YOUR EYE ON WHAT YOU'RE FIGHTING FOR, LITTLE GIRL...

"THAT SHOULD TELL YOU ALL YOU NEED TO KNOW ABOUT WHERE YOU'RE GOING."

TAKE ACTION!

SAVE THE COMMUNITY GARDEN!

SAVE OUR HOME!

0872-6X11

SAVE THE GARDEN

SAVE OUR COMMUNITY

SAVE OUR GARDENS
SAVE OUR COMMUNITY
YOU CAN MAKE A DIFFERENCE!
SIGN THE PETITION!
JOIN THE MOVEMENT!
MEETING UP TONIGHT!
JUSTICE TOGETHER
JUSTICE TOGETHER
JUSTICE

SAVE OUR COMMUNITY
SAVE OUR GARDEN
GARDEN CITY
GREEN
HEY.
HI.
YOU WEREN'T IN SCHOOL TODAY.
YEAH.
WE'RE HAVING A PROTEST TONIGHT.
SHE'S OUT HERE!
YEAH? THAT'S COOL.
JUSTICE TOGETHER
IT'S TO RAISE AWARENESS, BUILD COMMUNITY CONNECTION, TO PROTEST KANE ENTERPRISES.
BECAUSE WE'RE ALL IN THIS TOGETHER. HEY, HARLEEN.
HI, SIR.

HEY, IT'S A PARTY.
HEY, HARLEY.
IT'S THE BEGINNING OF AN ONGOING REVOLUTION. FLYER?
DON'T MIND IF I DO.
WE'RE HOPING WE CAN GET YOU TO JOIN US TONIGHT.
HEY. I GOTTA GO.
O-OKAY.
COMMUNITIES FIGHT FOR JUSTICE
WHAT'S THIS ABOUT?
HELLO! ARE YOU FROM MAMA'S?
OUR REPUTATION PRECEDES US.
ALSO WE ARE DESERVEDLY INFAMOUS.

Harleen-
Wish you were here! So happy to think of you with Grandma! finally making some $$$
See you in the Summer!
MoM XX
Harleen Quinzel
137 Broadward
Gotham
SOMETIMES LIFE IS LIKE A JAR OF COOKIES AND SOMETIMES IT'S A HIVE OF BEES AND SOMETIMES IT'S A PUZZLE WITH LOTS OF PIECES.
HARLEEN WAS NEVER BIG ON PUZZLES.
HEY, KIDDO, YOU LOOK LIKE YOU JUST GOT HIT WITH THE BUMMED-OUT TRUCK.
MAYBE TWO BUMMED-OUT TRUCKS.
SO, WE NEED TO FIGURE OUT A NEW PLAN. YOU SHOULD PROBABLY GET WORD TO YOUR MOM.
OKAY.
WHERE ARE YOU GONNA GO?
THAT IS A MYSTERY YET TO BE SOLVED, KIDDO. BUT DON'T WORRY ABOUT ME.
A QUEEN ALWAYS LANDS ON HER HEELS.
WHEN YOU FINALLY GET TO PACKING, I WANT YOU TO HAVE THIS.

DALI SAID IT WAS SOMETHING YOU LIKED. THE HARLEQUIN.
THANKS, MAMA.
I WISH WE COULD FIND A WAY TO ALL STAY TOGETHER, KIDDO. I DO WISH THAT.
I WISH THIS WASN'T HAPPENING.
THUMP THUMP THUMP
ME, TOO.
WHAT WAS THAT?
UH. I'LL CHECK.

HELLO? WHO'S BEEN THUMPING?
MY, WHAT A BIG BOW YOU HAVE.
YIKERS.
WHA?
HOW DO YOU GET INTO THIS THING?
AND WALK?

HARLEEN KNEW THAT CHEERLEADER OUTFITS WERE FOR CHEERLEADERS, WHO ARE MOSTLY FOR WHEN IT'S FIRST AND THIRD AND THE BALL IS WAITING TO BE KICKED BY SOME GUY WEARING BIG SHOULDERS AND FUNNY SHOES.
ALSO, SHE KNEW SOMETHING WAS NOT EXACTLY THE WAY IT SHOULD BE.
DUMP
JUSTICE TOGETHER
BUT SOMETIMES WHEN THINGS AREN'T RIGHT YOU GOTTA GO FIND A WAY TO MAKE THEM RIGHT.
R
MOST FAIRY TALES ARE STORIES WHERE THINGS AREN'T RIGHT.
RAGS

THE PROBLEM WITH MOST FAIRY TALES IS THAT PEOPLE WAIT AROUND FOR SOMEONE TO FIX THINGS FOR THEM.
IF YOU THINK ABOUT IT, MOST PEOPLE IN FAIRY TALES AREN'T THAT SMART.
LADIES EATING POISON APPLES.
LOONY GLUE
100% SUPER STRONG
WARNING
LITTLE KIDS WALKING INTO STRANGE COOKIE HOUSES.
RAGS
PRINCESSES NEEDING TO BE RESCUED.

PRAYING FOR MAGIC PUMPKINS.

HARLEY DIDN'T HAVE ANY MAGIC PUMPKINS.

BUT SHE HAD A MASK.
AND A FAIRY GODPERSON WHO NEEDED HER HELP.
AND SO...

PLEASE STAY WITHIN THE PERIMETER SET UP BY THE PEOPLE IN SAFETY VESTS.
WE WILL BE LEADING YOU THROUGH TRAFFIC.
IS EVERYONE READY TO SPREAD THE WORD? ARE YOU READY TO STAND UP FOR YOUR RIGHTS?
YEAH!
OUR HOME OUR
GO AWAY CORPORATE BULLIES
HARLEY HEADED INTO THE WOODS.
WE ARE GOING TO MARCH DOWN FIRST TO WAYNE STREET AND THEN ACROSS THAT TO FOURTH.
YOU KNOW, THE METAPHORICAL-TYPE WOODS.
YOU OKAY?
COMMUNITIES FIGHT FOR JUSTICE
YEAH, I JUST THOUGHT I SAW SOMEONE.
COMMUN
TO THE CASTLE.
THE OTHER, OTHER CASTLE.

THE EVIL KASTLE.
KNOCK-KNOCK.
WHO'S THERE?
SECURITY: MAIN DOOR
HARLEY.
HARLEY WHO?
SECURITY: MAIN DOOR
I HARLEY THINK THAT'S THE POINT.
SECURITY: MAIN DOOR

CAN I HELP YOU?
TRICK OR TREAT!
OKAY, VERY FUNNY, KID.
YA KNOW WHAT'S FUNNY?
SOME DING-DONG GUY THOUGHT I'D NEED A CHEERLEADER OUTFIT TO GET IN HERE!
OKAY, KID. NO MORE FUNNY BUSINESS.
THAT'S WHAT YOU THINK.

THE KEY TO KNOCKING OUT PEOPLE IS A SOLID WHACK TO THE NOGGIN.
HARLEEN LEARNED THAT IN A BOOK SHE GOT IN THE LIBRARY.
EDUCATION IS IMPORTANT.
STAY IN SCHOOL.
TA-DA!

WANNA KNOW SOMETHING WEIRD?
I FOUND THESE IN MY GRANDMA'S HOUSE.
MY GRANDMA WAS A COMPLICATED LADY.
BUT YOU EXPECT THAT WHEN YOU'RE A FAN OF CLOWNS.
HELLO!
SECURITY:REAR LOBBY
WHERE IS SHE?
HEY THERE! KNOCK-KNOCK!
YOU'RE LATE.
YOU'RE SUPPOSED TO SAY, "WHO'S THERE?"

YOU'RE NOT WEARING THE COSTUME I LEFT FOR YOU.
YEAH. IT WASN'T REALLY MY CUP OF MILK-SHAKE.
GRAB THE OTHER BAG.
WHAT'S IN THESE THINGS ANYWAY? ARE THEY SLEEPING BAGS? BALLOONS?
ALL IN GOOD TIME.
COMPUTER ROOM
HEY. UH, JOKER?
WHERE ARE WE GOING?
HURRY UP.

WHAT HAPPENED TO YOUR SHOES? YOU LOOK LIKE YOU WERE DANCING IN CHOCOLATE PUDDING. WERE YOU DANCING IN CHOCOLATE PUDDING?
NOTHING HAPPENED TO MY SHOES.
SUDDENLY, EVEN AFTER TAKING OUT TWO SECURITY GUARDS WITH HER BARE PAWS, THINGS DIDN'T FEEL REALLY SUPER ANYMORE. THEY FELT--
DING!
--WEIRD.
NOT GOOD WEIRD.
WARM-EGG-SALAD WEIRD. WEIRD LIKE--
GOING UP.

YOU KNOW, YOU SPEND TIME AND CARE CRAFTING A PLAN.
THERE'S AN ART TO IT. ORCHESTRATION. DIRECTION.
VISION.
I THOUGHT YOU SAID WE WERE GOING TO MESS UP THE COMPUTERS.
DID I?
YEAH, IT IS WHAT YOU SAID, MR. SO-CALLED SMARTY-BRAIN.
CHANGE OF PLANS.
WE FIGHT! FOR OUR HOME! WE FIGHT! FOR OUR RIGHTS!

THE PROTEST!
THEY'RE COMING THIS WAY.
OPEN SPACE
SAVE OUR CITY
SAVE OUR GARDENS
SAVE OUR COMMUNITY
PEOPLE FIRST
COMMUNITYS SUPPORT
LEAF US ALONE!
GREEN SPACES!
YOU CAN'T BLOW THE SIGN. IT'LL FALL ON THEM.
WILL IT NOW?
WELL, THAT WOULD BE QUITE SOMETHING, WOULDN'T IT?
I HAVE TO SAY, I THINK YOU'VE DRASTICALLY MISREAD THINGS, MISS QUINN.
MAYBE ***YOU'RE*** NOT THE SMARTEST CARD IN THE DECK.
GRAB 'ER.

IT WOULD HAVE BEEN AMUSING TO HAVE YOU ON TAPE IN YOUR LITTLE CHEERLEADER OUTFIT, BUT I BELIEVE WE'LL HAVE SUFFICIENT EVIDENCE OF YOUR GUILT.
THE TAPE OF YOU DOWN-STAIRS IN YOUR DOLLAR-STORE MASK.
AND WE'LL LEAVE YOU TIED UP ON THE ROOF, OF COURSE.
OH, HARLEY, DID YOU REALLY THINK THIS WAS YOUR *ALICE IN WONDERLAND*?
DON'T YOU KNOW THAT I AM THE GREAT AND POWERFUL **OZ?**
YOU'RE NOT SUCH A SMART GUY.

THE WIZARD OF OZ WAS JUST A DUMB OLD GUY HIDING BEHIND A CURTAIN.
AND YOU'RE A GUY IN A PLASTIC BAG ABOUT TO GET HIS BUTT KICKED.
SPEAKING OF CURTAINS.

JOHN KANE THE JERK?!
MISS QUINN.
FIGHT! FOR OUR HOMES! FIGHT! FOR JUSTICE!
THIS CHANGES NOTHING.
THE STAGE IS SET, MISS QUINN. FOR YOU AND LITTLE MISS IVY.
FIGHT! FOR OUR RIGHTS! FIGHT! FOR OUR FAMILIES!
OH, LITTLE MISS IVY...
...HOW WILL YOUR GARDEN GROW NOW?
IVY!

EVERYBODY!
EVERY-BODY RUN! THE SIGN! THE SIGN'S GONNA BLOW!
EVERYBODY RUN!
EVERYONE CLEAR OUT! EVERYONE MOVE!
CITY GARDEN
GREEN PLEASE
GREEN PLEASE!

ARE YOU OKAY?
IT'S KANE. KANE IS THE JOKER!
COMMUNITIES FIGHT FOR JUSTICE
HE SAID... THE JOKER SAID...
WHAT?
HE SAID--
YOUR GARDEN!
WHAT?
HE'S GOING TO BLOW IT UP!

WHAT IS HAPPENING?
HE BLEW UP THE SIGN. HE SAID SOMETHING ABOUT YOUR GARDEN!
BECAUSE IT'S YOUR SPECIAL THING.
AND HE'S A MEGA-ASSHOLE!
AND HIS SHOES WERE COVERED IN MUD.
COMMUNITY GARDEN
MAYBE HE WAS BACK BY THE WATERING SHED. IT'S SUPER MUDDY BACK THERE.
YOU HAVE TO CALL THE BOMB SQUADRON. CALL THE ROBOTS. CALL THEM ALL!

I'M GOING TO GET MY PARENTS.
DO NOT GO IN THERE.
GOT IT!
WILL DO!
OUR HERO...
MOM!
IVY!
SHE'D FOLLOWED JOHN KANE THE TOTAL PUTTHOLE INTO A TRAP.
WHAT COULD BE WORSE?
OTHER THAN MAYBE A TOENAIL SANDWICH.
OR A SNOT BUBBLE THAT NEVER GOES AWAY THAT YOU HAVE TO LIVE WITH YOUR WHOLE LIFE.
RIGHT.
ALL HARLEY COULD DO NOW WAS SAVE THE DAY. IT WAS THE ONLY CHOICE.

UH-OH.
WHAT TIME IS IT, MR. KANE?
MAYBE YOU'RE THINKING THIS IS THE PART OF THE FAIRY TALE WHERE LITTLE HARLEEN GETS BLOWN INTO TUNA FISH SALAD RIGHT THERE IN THE GARDEN SHED.
TICK-TOCK. TICK-TOCK. DEATH.

WHICH WOULD HAVE BEEN A PRETTY BIG BETTY BUMMER.
EVEN IF A PERSON ISN'T A PERFECT HERO...
...THAT'S NO REASON TO BLOW THEM UP.
CRICK!

HOLY CAPTAIN CRUNCHY! I'M ALIVE!
ALL RIGHT, HARLEEN! COME OUT WITH YOUR HANDS UP.
GUESS HARLEEN BEING DEAD LIKE A DOORNAIL WASN'T MEANT TO BE OR NOT TO BE.
SO...THIS IS ACTUALLY THE ONLY HARLEY-QUINN-SAVES-THE-DAY MOMENT YOU GET.
ENJOY IT.
PUT YOUR HANDS UP!
IT IS BIKINI BRIEFS.

I MEAN, YEAH, OBVIOUSLY NOT EVERYTHING ENDS UP HAPPILY EVER AFTER.
GET IN THERE!
CPD

EVERYONE BACK! I WANT EVERYONE BACK!
HARLEY!
OH, KIDDO!
COMMUNITIES FIGHT FOR JUSTICE
"EVER AFTER" MEANS INFINITY, AND WHO HAS THAT MUCH TIME TO TELL A STORY?
RIME
RIME SCENE DO NOT CROS

HANDS UP!
"HEAR YE! HEAR YE!"

ALL RISE FOR THE PRETRAIL THINGY OF THE APPARENTLY STUPID HARLEY QUINN AND THE TOTAL BOOGER, THE ULTIMATE SLIMEBALL...

...PRINCE JOHN KANE.

THE HONORABLY JUDGING ME PRESIDING.

THE CHARGES ARE RECKLESS ENDANGERMENT AND DESTRUCTION OF PROPERTY. HOW DO THE DEFENDANTS PLEAD?

HARLEY'S MOM WAS MAROONED ON A CRUISE SHIP IN THE MIDDLE OF THE DEEP BLUE SEA, SO SHE COULDN'T BE THERE.

THE PUBLIC DEFENDER PERSON SMELLED LIKE SOUR CREAM AND ONION CHIPS. WHICH ARE YUMMY.

NOT GUILTY, YOUR HONOR.

YOUR HONOR, MY CLIENT IS AN UPSTANDING MEMBER OF HIS COMMUNITY, WHO IS INVESTED IN THE SUCCESS OF HIS PARENTS' ENTERPRISE, WHY WOULD HE--

A **PLEA**, WHEN YOU'RE READY, COUNSELOR.

NOT GUILTY.

BAIL IS SET AT $500,000 EACH.

HEY?
YEAH, I'M AT THE COURTHOUSE. I'M JUST... YEAH. YEAH, GUESS WHO JUST POSTED HALF A MILLION DOLLARS BAIL?
HEY, PRINCE CANDY KANE, WHY'D YOU DO IT?
ME? WHAT DID I DO? I WAS JUST VISITING MY PARENTS AT WORK AND THEN YOU DRAGGED ME UP TO THE ROOF SO I COULD WITNESS YOU BLOWING UP THEIR PRECIOUS BUILDING.
YOU KNOW WHAT I THINK?
I THINK YOU'RE NO CHAOS PERSON. YOU'RE JUST A JOHN KANE.
FUNNY YOU DIDN'T FIGURE THAT OUT SOONER.
MAYBE THEN YOU COULD BE OUT THERE MAKING THE WORLD A BETTER PLACE WITH YOUR BUBBLY PERSONALITY INSTEAD OF GOING TO JAIL TO ROT.

YOU AND ALL THESE OTHER NOBODIES WILL ALWAYS BE MY PLAYTHINGS.
I'M A PLAYTHING?
WHAT ARE YOU?
I'M AN ENIGMA.
YOU'RE AN ENEMA?
HUH, JOHN KANE IS AN ENEMA. WHO KNEW?
ENIGMA!
SEE YA IN COURT, ***ENEMA!***

CHAPTER NINE

AND SO IT WAS, OUR HERO HARLEEN WAS FOILED BY A BOOGER.
AND SINCE SHE, UNLIKE PRINCE JOHN THE JOKER, HAD NO GOLD FOR BAIL...
...THEY SENT HER TO THE KLINKETY KLINK, A.K.A. THE HOLE, A.K.A. THE DEEP, DARK, DINGY DUNGEON, WHILE THE PRINCE HEADED BACK TO HIS CASTLE TO SIT ON HIS BUCKETS OF MONEY WITH A SPECIAL ANKLE BRACELET.
THE END.

WHAT HAVE WE LEARNED? WHAT IS THE MORALE OF THE STORY? WHERE DID I GET THIS PUDDING? ALL QUESTIONS YOU MAY BE ASKING YOURSELVES.
I THINK YOU MEAN MORAL?
WAIT. IS THIS STILL A RED RIDING HOOD THING?
YEAH, I FEEL LIKE YOUR STORY HAS A LOT OF UNRESOLVED LITERARY ALLUSIONS...
WHERE DID YOU GET THAT PUDDING?
WE LEARNED THAT BOOGERS, LIKE DEVILS, ARE SNEAKY.
SOMETIMES THEY WEAR THEIR BOOGERNESS ON THEIR SLEEVE, SOMETIMES THEY'RE A PAPER-BAG PRINCE IN DISGUISE.
LIKE THAT STORY ABOUT THE PRINCE WHO WAS A FROG!
SORT OF!

BEWARE A VILLAIN WHO SENDS YOU A POLYESTER TUTU SO YOU CAN DO HIS DIRTY BUSINESS.
AND THEN TRIES TO BLOW UP YOUR FRIENDS.
WHAT KINDA VILLAIN WEARS A TUTU?
THIS ISN'T ABOUT TUTUS! THIS IS ABOUT BOOGERS.
PRISONERS TO THEIR CELLS. LINE UP IN SINGLE FILE.

JOHN KANE.
YOU MIGHT BE A LIAR.
BUT I'M A MENACE.
SCRITCH SCRATCH
"SO...?"

SO. I GUESS... UH. HOW'S PRISON?
IT'S NOT SO BAD. THE COFFEE IS BAD, BUT THE PEOPLE ARE KIND OF NICE, BUT THE BEDS ARE BAD, BUT THE SOUP IS PRETTY GOOD.
BUT I MISS EVERYONE.
YEAH.
I MISS YOU, TOO.
I DIDN'T KNOW THE JOKER WAS A BOOGER.
THE BOOGER.
AND I CAN'T BELIEVE I'M STILL SAYING THAT WORD.
I SHOULD NEVER HAVE LISTENED TO HIM. HE SAID EASY STUFF LIKE, "LET'S GO BLOW UP THINGS." AND I WANTED TO MAKE THINGS BETTER. AND I WAS MAD. AND I LIKE BLOWING STUFF UP.
YEAH.
I KNOW--
MAN, I SPENT ALL THIS TIME THINKING ABOUT WHAT I WANTED TO SAY TO YOU.
I HAVEN'T REALLY SLEPT SINCE THAT NIGHT.

"YOU KNOW, I WAS ALWAYS WORRIED ABOUT BAD THINGS HAPPENING TO ME OR MY PARENTS.
RESIST
"JOHN KANE TRYING TO BLOW UP THE GARDEN, IT WAS LIKE, SO CLOSE, YOU KNOW?
"LIKE THE WORST THING ALMOST *DID* HAPPEN.
THEN THERE'S YOU, RUNNING INTO A BUILDING WITH A BOMB ABOUT TO GO OFF.
I WASN'T SCARED.
REALLY?
OKAY. MAYBE THIS MUCH.
YEAH.
WELL. *I'M* SCARED.
JOHN KANE DID WHAT HE DID SO HE COULD MAKE US LOOK LIKE CRIMINALS. SO THEY COULD JUSTIFY KICKING US OUT OF OUR NEIGHBORHOOD.
AND HE DID IT BECAUSE HE COULD.
YOU THINK IF SOMEONE FROM MY COMMUNITY TRIED TO BLOW UP A BUILDING WE'D BE OUT ON BAIL?
NO.

SO, IT'S A SYSTEM OF OPPRESSION AND WE HAVE TO FIGHT IT, BUT SOMETIMES I JUST WANT TO TAKE A BLOWTORCH TO KANE ENTERPRISES.
AND SOMETIMES I WANT TO DISAPPEAR.
BUT I WON'T. EVEN IF IT SEEMS HOPELESS, I CAN'T GIVE UP. BECAUSE THERE ARE THINGS WORTH FIGHTING FOR.
I'M NOT GIVING UP EITHER.
GOOD.
EVEN THOUGH IT'S TOTALLY STUPID AND KIND OF CRAZY THAT YOU RISKED YOUR LIFE, I WANTED TO THANK YOU FOR SAVING THE GARDEN.
AND...I THOUGHT YOU MIGHT GET A KICK OUT OF THIS.
I'M GOING TO TAKE HIS PRECIOUS FILM CLUB. I'M GOING TO TAKE IT AND MAKE IT RIGHT.
VOTE IVY FOR FILM CLUB PRESIDENT!
OOOOOO YEAH!
I MEAN, IT'S NOT EVERYTHING BUT--
THAT'S IT. WRAP IT UP, LADIES, VISITING HOURS ARE OVER.

IVY.

I...

YES?

THANKS. FOR COMING TO SEE ME.
I MEAN, OF COURSE. I'LL, YOU KNOW, COME BACK. BEFORE YOUR TRIAL.
OH YEAH.

MAMA SAID TO GIVE YOU THIS.

Dear Kiddo,
Just wanted to send a little note to let you know we queens over here are thinking of you. We are moving house but we are not giving up. We are fabulous and the world needs more of that right now.
Also, so you know, I'm pretty sure the world needs at least one Harley Quinn, so hang in there. You will always be part of this royal family of weird queers.
And no matter what happens, you will always have a home with this fairy. Let me know if you need some money for ramen noodles or soap.
xoxox
MAMA
HARLEY QUINN?
PRESENT.
JOKER SAYS HELLO.

SIT STILL.
EH, IT'S JUST A SCRATCH.
YOUCHERS.
-GROAN-
COOL SLING.
TELL THE JOKER HARLEY SAYS, "HI TO YOU, TOO."
I'M NOT THE LAST.
DUH.
FOOL ME ONCE, CHAMPAGNE ON ME.

KNOCK KNOCK

MRS. KANE?

JUST A SECOND, MARK, IT'S THESE RIDICULOUS AGENTS AGAIN.
CAN I HELP YOU?
THE ANKLE TRACKER SEEMS TO BE MALFUNCTIONING. AGAIN.
WHERE IS JOHN?
HE'S UPSTAIRS IN HIS ROOM, OF COURSE.
REALLY...THIS IS HARASSMENT. I'VE HALF A MIND TO CALL OUR ATTORNEY.
WE JUST NEED TO CONFIRM HIS LOCATION. WE ARE WORKING ON THE APPARENT BUGS IN THE SYSTEM, MRS. KANE.
JOHN? IT'S THE AGENTS AGAIN. PLEASE COME DOWNSTAIRS.
MMMM.
JOHN!

JOHN!
THAT'S A CODE YELLOW. SUSPECT IS AWOL. SUSPECT IS NOT IN THE NEST.

Hello, Mama. Prison is not as fun as drag.
I have spent a lot of time thinking...
...'bout what my mom said about there being two kinds of people.
I think it is more complicated than that.
I think people can be a lot of things. Things you don't expect.
I don't get all of it but I feel like I get a little more than I did a month ago.
~~I thought I could spot a booger from fifty yards away.~~
~~I was wrong.~~
Now I know that there are Jokers.
There are people who will do anything to get what they want.
~~My mom believes in angels.~~
~~I don't know if I do.~~
I might not know what I am but I know what I have to do.
And, Mama, if you ever need one...

...I will be your angel.
MAMA
MoM,
Do not worry.
I will be OK.
XO
Harleen
SCRITCH
SCRATCH
PERFECTO-MAMBO.
I'M COMING FOR YOU JOKER!
I'M YOUR DEVIL NOW.
XOXO
THANKS FOR THE PUDDING, PUDDIN'.

WAYNE ENTERPRISES
SHE BROKE OUT? IMPRESSIVE.
IT WOULD APPEAR SO.
I GUESS SENDING HER A LAWYER...WE'RE A LITTLE LATE ON THAT.
WELL, SIR, IF SHE GETS ARRESTED AGAIN, SHE WILL NEED A VERY GOOD LAWYER, SINCE JUDGES DON'T LOOK TOO KINDLY ON BREAKING OUT OF PRISON.
AND THE JOKER?
NO TRACE OF HIM YET.
MASTER WAYNE?
THAT'S ALL FOR NOW, ALFRED.
CAN YOU SEND IN LEGAL? AND MAXWELL FROM ACCOUNTING?

DRAG HERE!
OPEN!
19
OKAY, CHICKENS, ARE YOU READY FOR A LITTLE DEBAUCHERY DRAGGERY HATCHERY MIX-MATCHERY? I THINK YOU ARE.
THIS IS DRAG ON THE GO, MY FINE FEATHERED FRIENDS! WE ARE MAKING THE BEST OF DESPERATE TIMES.
WE WILL NOT BE RUN OUT OF TOWN AS LONG AS THERE ARE ABANDONED CHICKEN SHACKS.
ARE YOU READY FOR A LITTLE SONG?
WELCOME TO THE STAGE MISS DALI IN A DOILY!
YAS! WOOOT!

HELL YEAH, LET'S GET SOME BOWIE IN THIS HEN-HOUSE!
REBEL REBEL!
HEY, BABE!
HEY, MAMA.
HEY, KIDDO.
I'M GLAD YOU'RE NOT ALL SINGING SAD SONGS.
NOT TODAY. TODAY WE'RE FEELING PRETTY GOOD.
YAY.

YOU TAKE CARE NOW.
I WILL, MAMA.
LOVE YOU, KIDDO.
LOVE YOU, TOO.
DO DO DO DO DO DO DOO DO!
SEE YOU SOON.
OPEN!
DO DO DO DO DO DO DOO DO!

COUNCILLOR
CORRINE DU
COUNCILLOR DU?
MAYBE YOU SHOULD TAKE A LOOK AT THIS? A GUY IN A LIMO JUST DROPPED IT OFF.
IT'S...A DONATION.
FROM WHOM?
WAYNE ENTERPRISES.
REALLY? HOW MUCH?
A LOT.
HOLY SHIT!
IS THIS LEGAL?
LET'S MAKE SURE IT IS.
THIS COULD HELP WITH THE CHALLENGE TO KANE ENTERPRISES. THIS COULD SAVE THE GARDEN, RIGHT?
YES, IT COULD.

HERE, JOKER, JOKER, JOKER.
COME OUT, COME OUT...
...WHEREVER YOU ARE.
I'M COMING FOR YOU.
YOU BOOGER.

GET READY.
LET'S PLAY.

THE END

MARIKO TAMAKI

is an award-winning Canadian writer living in Oakland, California. She is the author of *Saving Montgomery Sole* and the co-creator, with Jillian Tamaki, of *This One Summer,* which received the prestigious Eisner and Ignatz awards as well as Caldecott and Printz honors, and *Laura Dean Keeps Breaking Up with Me* with Rosemary Valero-O'Connell. Her growing slate of critically acclaimed comics and graphic novels includes *Teenage Mutant Ninja Turtles, Tomb Raider, Adventure Time, She-Hulk, X-23,* and SUPERGIRL: BEING SUPER.

STEVE PUGH

is a British writer and artist, born and based in the Midlands of England. Recruited for DC's Vertigo imprint at its inception, he worked on both HELLBLAZER and ANIMAL MAN, and then the PREACHER spin-off SAINT OF KILLERS. He co-created, wrote, and drew *Hotwire* for Radical. He has illustrated dozens of series for Dark Horse, DC, and Marvel, as well as drawn the critically acclaimed, Eisner-nominated reinvention of THE FLINTSTONES.

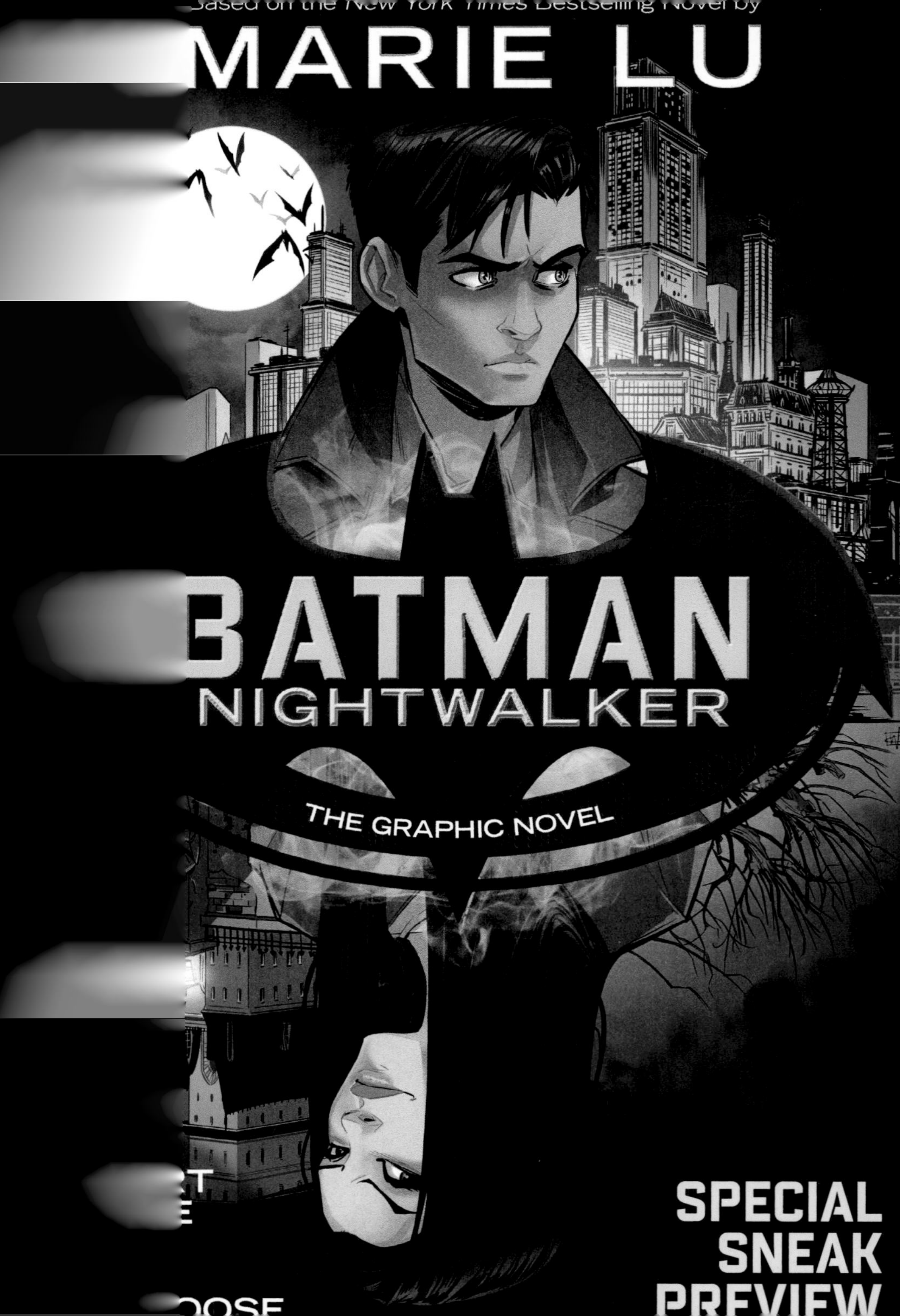
Based on the New York Times Bestselling Novel by
MARIE LU
BATMAN
NIGHTWALKER
THE GRAPHIC NOVEL
SPECIAL
SNEAK
PREVIEW

EXCERPT FROM BATMAN: NIGHTWALKER

ARKHAM ASYLUM?

I didn't know a madhouse could *be* a community service option.
I hear it's a nightmare inside.
Does Draccon really think it's okay to send you there? How are you supposed to study for finals?

You're actually studying? Most dedicated senior I know.
I'm serious, Bruce.
Arkham is dangerous, isn't it? Those prisoners are guilty of some of the most horrific crimes in Gotham City's history.

There are always jailbreaks and fights...

Sounds just like the rest of the world.

Harvey—you're staying the night, right?
If Alfred doesn't mind. But just tonight.
Dad'll expect me back tomorrow. He'll be sober by then.

You don't have to—
He's my *dad.*
And if I'm *not* there, I'll just make it worse for myself.

So did this detective say *why* she was sending you to a home for the criminally insane?
I think she wanted to teach me not to interfere with the police again.
I'll try to get on Draccon's good side. Maybe the whole thing won't be too terrible.

Well, at least you'll be able to say you've crossed paths with the most dangerous criminals in the city.
I mean, when will you get to do *that* again?

So I guess we're doing this.
I've been reading up on Arkham Asylum. Apparently it was always a controversial place.
When it opened its critics said that if it was a *prison*, it should be called one. If it was a *hospital*, it should be restructured with a ward, a mental health facility, and a rehabilitation center.
Asylums, they said, were relics of a darker time in history.
Maybe they were right. But I sure can't picture this place with flowering trees or green lawns.
Maybe...maybe it always looked like this.

Maybe it was always dying.
ARKHAM ASYLUM
Five weeks.

Five weeks in this hellhole.
Good luck, Master Wayne.
I'm sure they'll fly by.

Bruce, this is Dr. Zoe James. Head warden of Arkham.
You'll report directly to her.

The detective thinks I'm difficult. But we'll make this little visit of yours fun, Wayne.
You *are* difficult.
Don't make me regret this, James.

Mayor Price's administration keeps a very close watch over this place.
That should tell you how dangerous the city considers these criminals.
Here you go, kid.

Huh.
He don't look as rich as he does on TV.

My first thought is: *the walls are closing in.*
Feels like they're pressing closer and closer, getting ready to crush me like a bug.

Then I hear the screams.
Come on. Let's get this—

Echoes of angry shouts. A wild peal that might either be laughter or sobbing.
Well, well.
What's a delicate piece of flesh like you doing in a place like this?

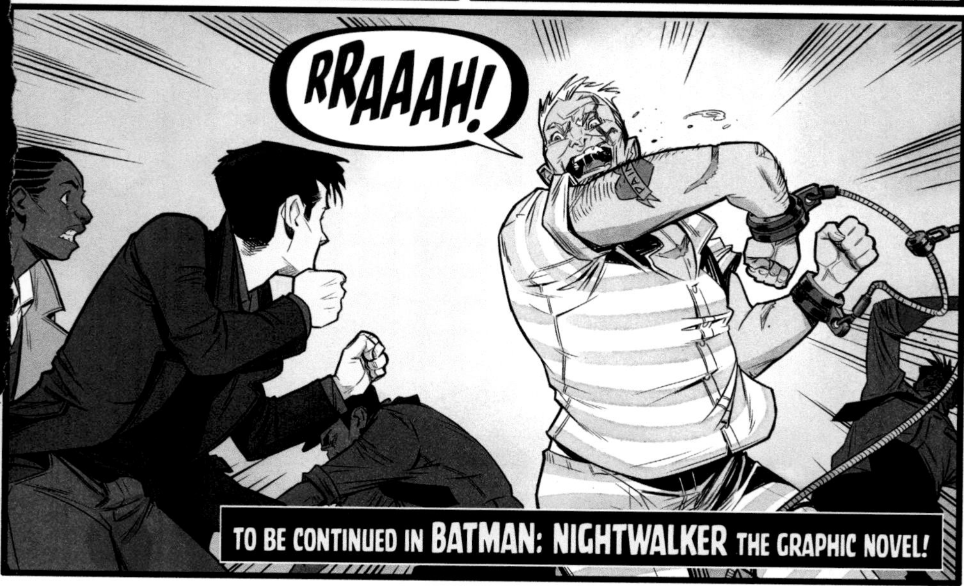
RRAAAH!
TO BE CONTINUED IN BATMAN: NIGHTWALKER THE GRAPHIC NOVEL!

COLOR